Angus Adams and Scream House

The Free-Range Kid Mysteries Book 3

Lee. M. Winter

ISBN: 1530814146

ISBN-13: 978-1530814145

DEDICATION

For Heather

CONTENTS

ACKNOWLEDGMENTS

Thank you to Beth at
www.bythebookediting.com

1 ZOMBIES!

The creature staggered forward. Angus backed away without taking his eyes from it. Arms outstretched for a gruesome embrace, (*dear God, it was missing fingers*), the thing chanted his name over and over and stared with undead eyes. Well, one un-dead eye to be precise. The other hung from its socket, lolling about crazily on a half-rotted cheek. Angus reached his own hands behind his back and grasped for the door handle he knew was there somewhere.

"Get back!" he shouted at the zombie thing. No reaction. Can zombies hear? Insanely, he tried to see if it had ears.

"I mean it!" *Yeah, that's it, tough guy, that should work. Tell the zombie you* mean *it.*

With blessed relief, his fingers felt the cool steel of the handle. He yanked the door open and turned, almost falling into the hallway before getting his legs and feet organised enough to run.

Reaching the stairs, he glanced back. The zombie was coming and it had picked up the pace. Angus bounded down the stairs two at a time and hurled himself at the front door, reefing it open.

"Arrgghhh!" A second zombie on the door step! It was smaller than the first but its mouth was open, as though stuck in an obscene yawn, revealing razor sharp, blood-dripping teeth. It lurched at him. He reeled back. *Think!* Okay, there's another door from the kitchen. Which way's the kitchen? Right. Go! Angus stumbled into a hall table, knocking a vase to the floor. From the corner of his eye he saw it smash, acutely aware that the big zombie had teamed up with its little pal and were both now staggering after him.

He raced into the kitchen and across to the far door.

The chanting zombie pair shuffled in behind him. Angus tried the door handle but it wouldn't budge. Locked! He rattled it harder, the way people do even when they know it's useless.

The zombies kept coming. He snatched up a broom from against the wall and held it out like a weapon.

"Don't come any closer!" he shouted and jabbed his broom at them to show he meant business (he had a broom and he wasn't afraid to use it). The zombies stalled, not coming any closer but still chanting. Wait. Did one of them just *giggle*?

There was a phone on the wall. Angus snatched it up and stabbed at the keypad, which was difficult to do without dropping the broom. He held the phone to his ear.

"No!" he shrieked into it, "you can't be dead!" He dropped the useless handset.

"Dead, dead, dead," the zombies sang in a horrific chorus. Together, they took a step closer, seemingly no longer afraid of the broom. Angus dropped it and rushed forward, pushing between them. The bigger zombie grabbed his shirt but he ripped it away and barged through. The front door was still open. He bolted for it, leaping over the shattered vase. As he passed through the doorway and into the garden he chanced a look over his shoulder. They were coming.

The sunshine was warm, and escape tantalisingly close. But not close enough. He tripped over an unfortunately placed potted geranium and went sprawling face-down in the dirt. With dread, he rolled over and stared into the faces of the undead.

The big one reached for him.

"Cut!" Bodhi lowered the camera. "Hamish, do you realise your costume still has the price tag on the back?" Hamish pulled off the zombie mask.

"What? You're kidding me?" He reached around, grabbing at the swinging tag. Bodhi snatched it off for him.

"We'll have to shoot the last part again. Without the price tag," she said. "But otherwise, that was pretty good. Angus, you really looked like you were about to poo your pants."

"Thanks," said Angus, getting up. "I've been studying up on pants-pooing faces. I think I've just about nailed it. The trick is to truly believe I'm being chased by zombies. Which is pretty easy…until one of them *giggles*, Liam?"

The little zombie pulled off his mask. Angus's

younger brother looked up at him. "Not me," he said.

"It was *me*," said Hamish. "Sorry, but you looked so funny waving that broom around like a lightsaber."

"We'll check the footage later and see if the giggle was picked up," said Bodhi. "If so we'll have to reshoot that part, as well. We need to concentrate, people. Submission date for the film festival is coming up."

"Is the kitchen clear of zombies?" called Mrs McLeod, Hamish's mother, from the doorway. "I thought you all might be hungry and in need of a wee snack." She shook her head. "Zombies. Of all the things to make a movie about. Hamish, you'll be having nightmares next, lad, mark my words."

They munched snacks in Hamish's room while his hero, Steve Irwin, grinned maniacally at them from half a dozen wall posters. From their terrarium, Frodo and Bilbo, the water dragons, also watched on, but with less grinning.

"You know what'd be really cool?" said Hamish. "We film the water dragons and then use the school's green screen to put the zombies in the shot, you know, so it'd look like they were going to be eaten by giant lizards."

"That's not a bad idea," said Angus. He reached for a

slice of watermelon. “Kind of Godzilla meets Zombies.” Hamish had never heard of Godzilla.

“Giant Japanese lizard from, like, the fifties,” said Bodhi. “But I thought we’d agreed our big ending would be a fiery pit with burning zombies writhing in agony?”

“I don’t want to writhe in agony,” said Hamish.

“You’d rather be eaten by a lizard?” said Bodhi.

“Well, yeah, that’d be cool. If you have to die, then it’d be quicker to have a giant lizard bite your head off than be cooked in a fire.”

“What if it didn’t bite your head off,” said Bodhi, wiping her hands on a napkin, “but ripped your stomach open instead and then chased you around with your guts hanging out?”

“I’d still prefer that over fire,” said Hamish, going for a second muffin. “I’m not good in the heat. It’s bad for my delicate Scottish complexion.”

Angus looked at his brother. Liam was staring intently at the water dragons. “What about you, Liam?” said Angus. “What would you rather do: burn up in a fire or be eaten by giant lizards?”

“Liam?”

“What?” Liam looked around.

“Would you rather burn in a fire or be eaten by

lizards?"

Liam shrugged and turned back to the terrarium. "Don't know. Whatever." Then he said, "Hamish, is it okay if I hold one?" Hamish took Frodo from the terrarium and passed him over. Liam gently stroked the dragon's head.

Angus studied his brother. At breakfast that morning, for the first time ever in the history of the universe, Liam had said 'no thanks' to Dad's bacon and eggs. And Angus hadn't had to tell him to shush up and leave him alone all week, *or* tell him to get out of his room, *or* fight with him for control of the TV remote, for that matter. What was going on?

"Okay," said Bodhi. "Just so we're clear, the first scene is you two playing Minecraft together. You're laughing about Minecraft Zombies when, suddenly, Hamish turns into one. A zombie, that is. Scene two, which we've just shot, is the chase inside the house where Angus discovers a second zombie, Liam, on the doorstep. He eventually escapes outside, but falls down, and it looks like the zombies are going to get him but he somehow gets away again. And scene three is the chase through a scary, overgrown garden where the zombies are finally lured into...what? Fiery pit or giant lizard enclosure?"

"Giant lizards," Angus and Hamish said, together.

Bodhi sighed. "Okay, lizards it is. But we still have to find a spooky garden. Any ideas, anyone?"

"Let's talk about it at school," said Angus, getting up.

Hamish walked them out. "Hey, the new teacher starts tomorrow."

"Yeah," said Angus. "I wonder what they'll be like." A new teacher was always a scary proposition. A good one made school a pleasure (well, *bearable*, at least) while a bad one could turn it into a living hell.

"This one's going to be good," said Hamish. "I can feel it in my waters."

"In your *waters*? What water? Where?"

Hamish shrugged. "I don't know, exactly. It's something Nanna says. But wherever my water is, I tell you it has a good feeling about this."

But Hamish and his waters were wrong.

Very wrong.

2 THE NEW TEACHER

Getting into class was slow going. A bottleneck of students had built up at the door and Angus, at the rear, wondered what the holdup could be. Finally, he made it in and understood. Next to him, Hamish uttered a quiet 'crikey'.

The desks had been aligned in perfect rows, all facing front, not one touching another. Previously, they'd been grouped so that four or five kids sat together. It was helpful for, well, group work. Not anymore.

"Stop gawking, find your name and sit down." The new teacher stood at the front of the room. He was middle-aged, bald, had closely set eyes, prominent nose, thin lips, and crossed arms. His tone brought immediate silence. Everyone exchanged looks as they searched for their seats. Angus found his, sat down, and watched the teacher's expressionless eyes follow individual students around the room.

"Too slow. I do not like waiting. You will do well to understand that," he said once all were seated. He began to pace back and forth across the front of the room.

"I am your new teacher. My name is Mr Beuglehole." He pronounced it 'bugle-hole'. "You, however, will call me 'Sir'. In this classroom you will not speak unless specifically instructed to do so. If you have a question, or information you wish to disseminate, you will raise your hand silently and wait for me to address you."

A couple of desks over, Perry took out his pocket notebook and start scribbling. Being a vocab nut who recorded every new word he heard, he was undoubtedly adding 'disseminate' to his list.

"You boy. What are you doing?" The teacher stopped pacing to glare at Perry. He looked up from his notebook, startled.

"I…er…" he stammered.

"You mean, '*Sir*, I…er…' don't you, boy?"

"I…yes, Sir. I like to write down new words." Perry looked about him as though hoping to spot an escape hatch.

Mr Beuglehole yelled, "I LIKE TO WRITE DOWN NEW WORDS, *SIR*!"

Perry jumped in his seat with everyone else. His face turning crimson, he said, in a voice so quiet it was almost a whisper, "I like to write down new words, Sir." His hands shook as they clutched the notebook.

"This was something encouraged by your last teacher, was it? Speak up, boy!"

"Um…yes. Yes, Sir. Miss Kirkland thought it was a good idea. Sir."

"What's your name, boy?"

"Um…Perry Pritchard, Sir."

"Well, listen carefully, *Perry Pritchard*, and this also goes for the rest of you. I will say this once. *Miss Kirkland* is no longer your teacher. *Miss Kirkland* has gone. I am not interested in how things were done when

Miss Kirkland was here. *I* am here, now. Do you all understand?"

No one said anything.

"DO YOU ALL UNDERSTAND?"

"Yes, Sir!" said the class all together.

"Good. Now, Pritchard. You can record new words in your own time. I will not be interrupted in class by you scratching about in that book. Is that clear?"

"Yes, Sir." Perry looked as though he might cry.

"Alright," said Mr Beuglehole, now pacing between the rows of desks. "You will all note the new weekly timetable on the wall. Please note, in particular, that in addition to our daily maths class there will be a mathematics 'intensive' every Friday from nine-thirty until ten-thirty followed by a quiz."

But that was when Angus and Hamish usually went to the robotics lab. Robotics was technically an extra-curricular activity but it had always been school policy that those involved could go during class time if nothing else too important was happening and the class teacher agreed. Angus and Hamish exchanged looks.

Mr Beuglehole *(what kind of name was that, anyway?)* had moved on. "Now," he said, "we are beginning a new history unit. This term, you will be studying Australia's early settlers. Please take out your history work books, turn to a new page, and rule a red margin precisely two point five centimetres from the left hand edge."

Angus tentatively raised his hand.

"Yes, boy, what is it?" The teacher stopped pacing.

"Sir, may I please ask a question about the timetable for Friday?"

"Make it fast."

"Well, you see, Sir, some of us attend robotics at nine-thirty on Fridays. Miss Kir–" Angus could have bitten off his tongue. He couldn't believe he'd almost said 'Miss Kirkland'. He prayed that Mr Beuglehole had missed it.

He hadn't.

"Are you stupid, boy?"

"Ah…I…" Angus didn't know what to say. *Seriously, how do you answer that?*

"I think you must be stupid. Correct me if I'm wrong but did I not just explain my feelings concerning Miss Kirkland?"

"Ah…yes, Sir." Angus tried to maintain eye contact *and* not simultaneously wet his pants.

"And what do you recall me saying about her?"

"Um…that she has left, Sir."

"And?"

"And, that you're not interested in how things were when she was here, Sir."

"Correct. So you heard all of that and yet chose to ignore it." The man strolled casually, hands behind his back, and stood directly in front of Angus. "So, let me ask you again: Are you stupid?"

Angus swallowed and said, "Sir, robotics is important–"

"You will not tell me what is important in this classroom. What is your name, boy?" Before Angus could answer the teacher looked at the desk label.

"Angus Adams," he said. The thin lips stretched into a smirk. "See me at first break, Mr Adams."

3 SCREAM HOUSE

At the bell, Angus waited for everyone to leave before he approached Mr Beuglehole's desk.

"Excuse me, Sir, you wanted to see me?"

The teacher placed his pen down slowly and looked at Angus. The moment dragged on and became awkward. Finally, he said, "I've heard about you, Adams. You think you're some kind of hero?"

What? Angus had recently received a bravery award for pulling a man from a burning building, but he certainly didn't go around thinking he was a hero. He didn't even like to talk about it, to be honest.

"Sir, I–"

"I don't like people, especially children, who are too big for their boots. You think you're some kind of hot shot? Be warned that I won't tolerate *attitude* in my classroom. Just watch yourself this term, Adams. Are we clear?"

"I–"

"*Are we clear?*"

"Yes, Sir."

***

Angus took his lunchbox and sat with the boys. The mood was subdued. Perry still looked close to tears.

"So, what did Trumpet-Butt want?" asked Finn, grinning. That did the trick. You could always rely on Finn for comic relief. Hamish laughed so hard he snorted, almost choked on a grape, and had to pull out his asthma puffer.

"Trumpet-Butt!" he said, between puffs, "that's perfect."

"I don't get it," said Perry.

"Trumpet. You know, like 'bugle'," Finn explained, patiently. "Beuglehole equals Trumpet-Butt."

"Oh, yeah, sure. That's funny," said Perry, as though it wasn't funny at all.

"Don't worry, Perry," said Angus. "I think he's going to pick on me more than you. Apparently, I'm too big for my boots."

Hamish put his puffer away. "What did he say about robotics?"

"He didn't. I guess we'll need to go and see Mrs Nesbit and tell her we can't come anymore. Maybe she'll talk to him."

As they ate, the discussion turned to the school film festival. Entering was optional. 'Lip-synced Music Video' was always the most popular category because you could create one easily using an iPad. That was fine, but Angus enjoyed the challenge of a scripted drama shot with a high-definition camera.

"The zombie thing sounds cool," said Finn, who had teamed up with Luke to make a spy comedy. "Where are you shooting it?"

"Actually, we need a scary garden. Know any?"

Finn thought for a moment. "What about Scream House?" He narrowed his eyes. "If you've got the guts, that is."

Scream House. *Of course*.

"Oh, yeah," said Hamish, "Scream House would be awesome." Then his face fell. "But what about old Mrs Screen?"

"What's Scream House?" asked Perry.

Finn rolled his eyes. "Don't you know anything? It's that enormous place on Birch Street. Big old mansion. Huge overgrown yard. Some old lady called Mrs Screen lives there. No one ever sees her but she's supposed to be filthy rich. Loads of money hidden away. Probably under the floorboards."

Angus laughed. "That's rubbish," he said. "About no one seeing her, anyway. She's one of Dad's customers. He's seen her a few times. I don't know about the filthy rich part."

"Why is it called '*Scream* House'?" asked Perry.

Angus shrugged. "That's just what everyone calls it. There used to be this sign on the gate that said 'Screen House' but '*Scream* House' suits it better because it's old and creepy looking."

"And it's haunted, of course," said Finn.

Hamish's eyebrows shot up. "Really?"

"It is not," said Angus. *Honestly, the rubbish some people believe.*

"Well, I've heard that it is," Finn insisted. "Mrs

Screen's daughter died there a few years ago." Then he added in a scary voice, "*but she never left…*"

***

Angus and Hamish were putting away their lunchboxes when Mr Jackson, the school groundsman, approached them. He was doing some volunteer work at the local community center, he said, running a free soccer clinic for little kids from disadvantaged homes. Could the two of them help out that afternoon? Angus looked at Hamish. They'd once thought Mr Jackson to be scary and intimidating, as he'd recently returned from being a soldier in Afghanistan. But since then, he'd helped them out of a few sticky situations and they not only respected him, but genuinely liked him. "Sure," said Angus.

"If it's going to be a regular thing, I'll have to check with my parents," said Hamish, "but I can come this afternoon."

"Great," said Mr Jackson. "See you then. Oh, and that friend of yours, Bodhi. She's good with a ball. Invite her along, too, if you like."

They watched him walk away. "You know, Scream House isn't far from the community center. Why don't we go there first and ask if we can film in the yard? It really is the perfect location."

"What about the haunted thing?" said Hamish.

Angus looked at him. "You're kidding, right?"

***

At a quarter to four, they stood on the quiet street outside Scream House. The gate was an old fashioned, wrought iron type. Beyond it, a cracked concrete path led up to the front door of the huge old house. At least it looked as though it did. It was hard to tell as the path disappeared beneath a jungle of overgrown shrubs and bushes. Also, large trees with low hanging branches made the house difficult to see clearly from the street.

"Come on," said Angus. He pushed open the gate. It screeched out an eerie protest. "Watch out for ghosts," he said, going in. Hamish giggled nervously, but followed.

The path meandered through the dark, shadowy garden and they had to use their hands to push back branches as they went. Although it was neglected and rundown, you could see that once upon a time the yard and house must have been spectacular.

Other than the whispering of the wind, everything was quiet. Around a turn a startled magpie flapped from the undergrowth. Hamish jumped.

"This place gives me the willies," he said, rubbing his bare arms although it wasn't cold. "No wonder it's called 'Scream House'."

They stopped briefly to look at a small clearing in which an old birdbath, discoloured with mould, had toppled and broken.

"You sure your dad has met this lady?" asked Hamish, as they continued on.

"I think so," said Angus. "Anyway, a creepy yard and house is always a red herring."

"A what?" Hamish pulled his shirt free from a clawing branch.

"A red herring. You know, in movies and books," said Angus, "you're always made to believe that the owner of the creepy old house is a horrible, evil, old witch, or whatever, and then they turn out to be really nice. I bet Mrs Screen is lovely. Probably invite us in for milk and cookies."

Just ahead, the bushes rustled and an old lady stepped onto the path.

"WRONG! I AM A HORRIBLE, EVIL, OLD WITCH AND I DON'T LIKE VISITORS."

4 THE TREE

"Arrgghh!" Hamish shrieked and grabbed Angus's arm.

"NOW CLEAR OFF BEFORE I PUT YOU IN THE DUNGEON!"

They turned and fled back along the winding path through the bushes, out the gate and onto the street. They kept running to the corner, where, puffing hard, they stopped and looked at each other.

"Crikey," said Hamish, breaking into a huge grin. Angus started to laugh. He couldn't help himself. Mrs Screen had well and truly scared the daylights out of them. Hamish started to laugh too. It really was just too funny. Angus laughed until his sides ached and tears rolled down his cheeks. It was a couple of minutes before they had themselves together enough to start for the community center.

Up the street they ran into Bodhi. "How'd you go with Mrs Screen? Is she going to let us film in her garden?" she asked.

"Um, the answer to that would be 'no'," said Angus. They told her what had happened.

"Perhaps you frightened her first," said Bodhi, "creeping around her garden like that."

"We weren't creeping. We were trying to find the front door!" said Hamish. "I don't know what else we could have done. Called out from the gate? Sent in a messenger pigeon first?"

Angus looked down the hill to the playing field of the community center. "Come on, we're late."

The three of them ran to the equipment shed where Mr Jackson stood with a group of young kids and parents. They were all looking at the shed. Angus skirted around them to get a better look. *Wow.* Across the front of the shed doors, 'LEAVE THE TREE ALONE!' had been spray painted in large, bright-green letters.

"Okay, everyone, let's not get distracted by this," Mr Jackson said. "We'll get started. Thank you all for coming. Angus, can you guys help me with the balls and cones?"

In the shed, Mr Jackson handed each of them some equipment.

"Who wrote that on the doors?" asked Angus, picking up a large bag of balls. "And what tree are they talking about?"

"It's nothing for you to worry about." Mr Jackson passed Bodhi a stack of cones. "The center's just having a small dispute with one of the neighbours over a dangerous tree, that's all."

Outside the shed, Hamish pointed across the playing field. "Is that the tree?" An enormous, half-dead ironbark stretched out from the other side of the fence, overhanging the field.

"Yes, that's the one," said Mr Jackson. "It needs to come down before it falls down and hurts someone."

"So, why won't the owner cut it down?" asked Bodhi, looking at the tree.

Mr Jackson shrugged. "That part's not clear. But as you can see from the shed door, they feel pretty strongly about it. Anyway, let's get started."

Mr Jackson began placing cones on the ground.

Hamish beckoned Angus and Bodhi to come closer. "You know whose tree that is, don't you? Whose *yard* that is?"

"Yes," said Angus. "Mrs Screen's."

The three of them stared at the tree. Beyond it, deep in shadow, Scream House stared back.

***

Angus tapped the ball to the little girl standing opposite. She did a good job of stopping it with her foot before kicking it back. "Good," he said, "but remember to use the side of your foot, like this." He demonstrated and passed the ball back to her. All the kids were practising passes. All except for one.

A small boy, about five years old, stood apart from the group. He'd lined up the spare balls neatly to one side and appeared to be counting them. Over and over again, he walked along his row of balls, his lips moving silently as he pointed to each ball in turn. Occasionally he stopped to adjust the position of one or another before resuming his counting. At drink break Angus went over to him.

"Hi," he said. "I'm Angus. What's your name?" The boy didn't reply, but just kept counting the balls.

Mr Jackson appeared at Angus's shoulder. "This is Ben. My son." Angus knew that Mr Jackson's young daughter had died a few years ago. He hadn't known he had a son, too.

"Ben doesn't talk. He's a bit different from other kids. He doesn't really like playing with others. Prefers to do his own thing."

Ben carried on as before, walking and counting silently. A small girl tugged at Mr Jackson's sleeve and took his attention.

Angus squatted, eyelevel with Ben. "That's a great line of balls you've got there. Can I count, too?" No answer. Angus walked along the row behind Ben, counting the balls aloud. "One, two, three, four, five." Then he stood behind the first ball and tapped it with the side of his foot. As it rolled away from the line he said, "Oh, no! It's getting away! Quick, get it back!" He rushed after it, grabbed it and put it back in line. Ben had stopped counting to stare at Angus.

Mr Jackson called out, "Angus, that's not a good idea—"

But Angus had already kicked the next ball and was chasing after it. "Quick, quick, it's getting away!" he said, grabbing it and placing it neatly back in line.

Ben laughed.

Mr Jackson closed his mouth and looked from Ben to Angus. Angus kicked the next ball and before he could say "Quick, get it" Ben darted after it himself, laughing out loud. He grabbed the ball, put it back in its place and then kicked the next one. And so the game continued.

Mr Jackson scratched his head. "Well, I'll be."

***

The soccer clinic finished and the younger kids left with their parents. Hamish's mother arrived to take him to chess club. It was the latest extra-curricular activity she'd signed him to, being a firm believer that kids needed an endless line-up of structured activities to keep them out of trouble. Angus knew many parents just like her. It continued to surprise him how many adults failed to see that just mucking about with your mates, climbing a tree, or simply sitting and pondering why you can't tickle yourself, were also good for you.

Bodhi left with Hamish. Angus offered to take Ben to the playground next to the center while Mr Jackson finished some paperwork.

"Does he like the swings?"

"Loves them. You might be sorry you offered, but that'd be great, thanks."

Angus took Ben's small hand and they turned toward the playground.

"Oh, Angus," called Mr Jackson, "Make sure you

shut the gate. Sometimes Ben runs off without warning."

***

In the playground, with the gate firmly shut, Angus pushed Ben on the swing. Its hinges groaned and complained with each push, reminding him of the gate at Scream House. On impulse he looked over at it. A curtain in a top window twitched.

Someone was watching.

5 ANOTHER MESSAGE

“**M**urphy! Six times nine?”

“Ah, fifty-four, Sir.”

“Pritchard! Eleven times eight?”

“Eighty-eight, Sir.”

“Adams, thirteen times nine?”

“Ah…um…” *What? Thirteen times nine?* Angus tried desperately to work out the answer but wasn’t fast enough.

“Not good enough, Adams. In addition to your

regular homework tonight, you will write out your thirteen times table. Ten times."

The rest of the school day continued in a similar fashion. Mr Beuglehole allocated new 'jobs'. Layla would be in charge of library book returns, Finn would collect class notes from the office, Hamish would answer the telephone, and Angus would put all the chairs on the desks at the end of the day. *After* the bell had rung and *after* everyone else had gone home.

Just before lunch, Luke and Perry tussled over a puzzle and it fell on the floor. The lid came off and puzzle pieces scattered.

"Adams, pick that up," said Mr Beuglehole. Angus had been standing nowhere near Perry and Luke.

"But, Sir, I didn't drop it," he said, knowing that saying so wouldn't make a scrap of difference. Trumpet-Butt walked over and looked down at the lid of the box.

"Apparently there are three-hundred pieces in this puzzle, Adams. Count them as you pick them up. Out loud. So I can hear you."

***

The three o'clock bell dragged its heels. Angus kept checking the clock, at one stage convinced it was running backwards. When the bell finally rang, and after he'd put up all the chairs, he rode his bike to the community center. Mr Jackson's car was already there. He rested his bike against the shed wall. Ben appeared and grabbed him around the leg in a ferocious hug.

"Hey, Ben. How're you going?"

Mr Jackson came from the building. "He's really taken a shine to you, hasn't he? Thanks for lending a hand. I've got scrubbing brushes and soapy water ready to go."

Angus soaped up his brush and together they started to scrub at the paint on the doors. Nearby, Ben lined up his soccer balls and silently played the kick-and-chase game.

From across the field someone began shouting.

"VANDAL!" It was Mrs Screen. Her back gate opened directly onto the sporting field and she stood there underneath the overhanging ironbark.

"THIS IS PURE VANDALISM!"

Mr Jackson dropped his brush into the bucket. "Excuse me, Angus," he said and strode off across the field. Angus followed. This was too interesting. He had to find out what was going on.

"Hello, Mrs Screen," said Mr Jackson, reaching the elderly lady. "What seems to be the problem?"

"You know exactly what the problem is," she said. Then her face crumpled. "Why are you doing this to me?" Her eyes were red and watery, as though she'd been crying. She clasped her shaking hands tightly together.

"I'm not doing anything to you, Mrs Screen. I promise you." Mr Jackson spoke kindly. "Tell me, what is the matter?"

"Look at my tree." She turned toward the overhanging tree, moving aside to let them look through the gate. Over the broad trunk of the iron bark, someone had spray-painted, "THE TREE MUST GO!" in big, red letters.

"Someone did this during the night," said Mrs Screen, in a trembling voice. "Who would it be, if not you?"

"Mrs Screen, I—"

"You've made it clear you want the tree gone. But is this *really* necessary? Who's going to clean this off?"

"Mrs Screen, it wasn't me. And I honestly can't imagine anyone from the center doing this." Mr Jackson scratched his head.

"Rubbish," said Mrs Screen. "Let me tell you—" She stopped talking to look at Ben.

He'd followed them over and was tugging at his father's pants, looking up with big eyes.

Mrs Screen stared at Ben for a long moment, her eyes wide, too. It was as if she'd forgotten what she was saying. She refocused. "I don't know why you want to hurt me like this," she said before turning and hurrying back through the gate. It shut with a loud clang.

Mr Jackson put his hand on his son's shoulder and sighed. "Come on," he said to Angus.

They went back to scrubbing the doors, Mr Jackson making it clear he didn't want to talk about Mrs Screen or her tree. Ben went back to his balls. They'd almost finished when someone else called from across the field.

"EXCUSE ME! HELLO?" This time it was a younger woman. She came through Mrs Screen's gate toward them.

"Hello, I'm Janet." She held out her hand to Mr Jackson. She was Mrs Screen's housekeeper, she said. She lived in the house and took care of the cooking and cleaning.

"I just wanted to meet you and talk about the tree. She's very upset."

"I know," said Mr Jackson. "But I didn't deface her tree and I don't know who did. And I also know that

Angus and I are busy here scrubbing clean our shed."

"Yes," said Janet. "I see that. This whole business is really getting out of hand."

"The tree *is* dangerous," said Mr Jackson. "I have the safety of the kids to think of."

"Yes, of course. But the tree holds great sentimental value to Mrs Screen. She really loves it. You see—"

"Look, thank you for coming by but I need to get packed up now, if you'll excuse me?" Mr Jackson walked away with Ben. Angus was left looking at Janet. She smiled.

"Angus, is it? Were you one of the boys who came by yesterday?"

"Yes. That was me and my friend, Hamish," said Angus. "We're sorry. We didn't mean to upset Mrs Screen." He went on to explain they'd been hoping she'd let them shoot a movie scene in her garden. "Anyway, it doesn't matter. We'll find somewhere else."

"No, no. You don't have to do that," said Janet. She glanced over her shoulder back at the house. "Mrs Screen's been unwell lately, that's all. I know you probably won't believe me, but she *is* very nice, usually. Look, she takes naps most afternoons and sleeps like a log. You're most welcome to come and use the yard if you still want to."

"Well, okay, we'll think about it. Thanks," said Angus. He glanced over at the house. It didn't look keen on the idea.

6 RAPATA

Angus tried Skyping Hamish as soon as he was home. There was no answer. Probably still at piano lesson, or debating club or wherever it was he went Wednesday afternoons. So instead, he sat at his desk and started writing out the thirteen times table. No point putting it off. Two minutes into it he heard shouting from downstairs. It was certainly the day for shouting. He went to investigate.

The hullabaloo was coming from the kitchen.

"Carry on all you like, Liam," his mother said. "You can wait for dinner. It's almost ready and you've already had two crackers, an apple, and a glass of milk."

"BUT I'M SO HUNGRY! IT'S NOT FAIR!" Liam stamped his foot, burst into tears, and ran past Angus and up the stairs.

Mum looked at Angus. "What on Earth is going on with your brother, lately?"

He shrugged. "I don't know. He won't talk to me."

His mother turned back to grilling the fish. Over her shoulder she said, "He won't talk to me either except to scream at me hysterically. And he's either refusing to eat because he feels sick, or else he's ravenously hungry, as though he hasn't been fed for weeks. I don't know what to do with him." She handed Angus a head of broccoli. "Can you chop this, please, love? And pop it into the microwave for me? The fish is almost ready."

***

After dinner Angus completed the ridiculous homework and, with an aching hand, Skyped Hamish again. He told him about Mrs Screen's tree.

"You know what I think?" said Hamish. "I think she did it herself."

“Did your waters tell you that?”

“Funny. No, seriously, I reckon she’s trying to get sympathy or attention or something.”

Angus considered this. It seemed unlikely. “Well, anyway, what do you think about filming in her yard, like that Janet lady suggested?”

Hamish paused then said, “I’m not sure we should. You know, without Mrs Screen saying it’s okay. I don’t want to be screamed at again like that.”

“Yeah, that’s what I think, too,” said Angus. “Hey, don’t forget to bring your zombie costume to school tomorrow. I’ll have the camera.”

***

Next day in the hall, they set up the school’s green screen. Mr Dingwall, the principal, had given Angus permission to use it on the condition that he was very careful.

“Okay,” said Bodhi, attaching the camera to the tri-pod. “I want the zombies dashing about frantically in front of the green screen. Well, as frantic as zombies can dash, anyway. Remember, you’re being chased by giant zombie-eating lizards.” She looked up from the tri-pod. “Okay, I’m ready. Where’s Liam?”

“He should be here,” said Angus. “I told him to come

as soon as the play bell rang." He peered out the door.

Bodhi looked over his shoulder. "There he is," she said.

"Where?" There were dozens of kids in the school yard, running, playing, chatting in groups.

"Over there behind the library. Wait. Is that Rapata with him?" Yes, down the hill at the library, Liam was standing in the shadow of Rapata Takani, a boy that had been causing problems for Angus since his schooling began. Rapata was an enormous hulk of a boy. Liam was dwarfed by him.

"What's he doing with Rapata?" said Hamish, also staring. As they watched, Liam said something and pointed up to the hall. Rapata turned and stared at Angus and the others. Smirking, he turned back and said something that caused Liam to burst into tears.

"I'm going down there." Angus strode from the hall and started down the hill with Hamish and Bodhi behind him. At the same time Rapata began walking up the hill.

They met halfway. Neither slowed down, but Rapata swerved his body as he passed and his shoulder knocked hard into Angus. "Watch where yer goin', Adams," he said. Angus stumbled but kept walking, saying nothing.

Liam was still crying when he got to him. "What's

wrong, Liam?"

"Nothing."

"Really? Why are you crying then? And what were you doing with Rapata?" Liam sniffed but otherwise remained silent and looked at his feet.

Bodhi bent down. "Liam. You can tell us. Honestly, you can."

Liam threw back his head. "I can't tell you! Leave me alone!" With a choking sob he pushed past them and ran off.

They watched him go.

"What are we going to do about filming?" asked Hamish.

"Let's try to get some done with just one zombie," said Bodhi. "We'll worry about Liam's part later."

They'd started to trudge back up the hill when Angus looked up to see Rapata leaving the hall. "Oh, no. Quick!" He broke into a run.

Charging into the building he immediately saw the green screen on the floor in a heap. It had been ripped from the stand, which now lay on its side, bent out of shape as though someone had jumped on it. Someone heavy.

Bodhi and Hamish followed him in. "Rapata!" said

Angus. “This is bad. What will we tell Mr Dingwall? I gave him my word I’d be careful with this.”

“Maybe we can fix it,” said Hamish.

Bodhi picked up a corner of the green fabric. “I don’t think so,” she said, holding it up. The screen had been ripped in half.

There was movement at the door and a deep voice bellowed, “What’s going on here? You three! Get away from that!” They jumped back. It was Mr Beuglehole. He strode over and looked at the broken screen. Squinting his already beady little eyes, he spoke slowly. “The three of you are in big trouble.”

7 THE MARBLES

"It wasn't us," said Angus. "We were about to use it. Mr Dingwall gave me permission, but..."

"But what? Out with it, Adams!"

"But...well, we left it alone for a couple of minutes and when we came back it was like this." This wasn't going well.

"You left it alone? You were given permission to use an expensive piece of school equipment and you *'left it alone'*? The three of you can go to the principal's office immediately."

They tried their best to explain to Mr Dingwall that they'd seen Rapata leaving the hall, that it was most likely he who'd done the damage. To his credit, the principal said he'd question Rapata but that didn't change the fact that the equipment was now ruined beyond repair or that the three of them had acted irresponsibly. Mr Dingwall said he was especially disappointed with Angus. "I expected better of you," he said.

The trip to the office made them late for class. Although Mr Beuglehole had sent them there in the first place he still put both their names on first reminder. Hamish argued back and had his name moved all the way to lunch time detention.

***

The final bell rang. Angus put up all the chairs, got his bag, and headed to the bike rack. On his way he passed Mr Jackson's workshop.

"Angus! Hey, you got a minute?"

The groundsman sat at his workbench. As always, it was covered with an assortment of broken computers and phones in the process of being repaired, to be donated to the Children's Hospital.

“Mate,” he said, “I’ve got a bit of a proposition for you. I’m taking on a few extra tasks down at the community center. After school stuff. I was wondering if you’d be able to watch Ben for me, just for a few afternoons? At the playground? Paid, of course. If your parents are okay with it.”

“Oh, okay, sure,” said Angus. Then something occurred to him. “What about Ben’s mother? She’s never met me. Will she mind?”

Mr Jackson looked down. “Ben’s mother died when he was born, Angus.”

“Oh, I’m sorry, I—”

“It’s okay. You weren’t to know.” He picked up the photo of his daughter and looked at it. Angus already knew that she had died, too, but Mr Jackson had never said how.

“I was overseas in the army when my wife was expecting Ben. I was supposed to be back in time for the birth, but he decided to arrive early.” Mr Jackson gave a little laugh. “He’s always in a rush, that kid. Anyway, my wife had to go to hospital in the middle of the night. My daughter was in the car, too. It was raining and they had an accident. Ben was born but the doctors couldn’t save my wife. My daughter was in hospital for a long time, but then she...well...you know that part. Anyway, now it's just me and Ben."

Angus didn't know what to say. That was the saddest story he'd ever heard. "I'd love to take Ben to the playground," he said. "But I don't want any money, thanks. Ben's a great kid. I'm happy to do it."

***

The playground was busy. A couple of mothers sat at a picnic table and chatted while their toddlers played in the sandpit. A few others sat on the available benches and watched older kids.

Mr Jackson hadn't been kidding about Ben loving the swings. He almost had a major meltdown when they were occupied. Luckily, Angus had thought ahead and brought a couple of soccer balls with him. They played the line-up-the-balls-then-kick-and-chase-them game for ten minutes or so until a swing became vacant and Ben threw himself onto it. Angus pushed him until his arms ached. *Did this kid never get tired of swinging?* Eventually, Angus insisting it was time for them to sit on a bench and eat the snacks Mr Jackson had packed.

Ben munched his mini Oreos and drank his water. Angus looked over at the nearby skate-bowl (there was a kid on a scooter doing incredible 360s) then became aware that someone had approached the bench.

It was Mrs Screen, of all people. She stood there looking at him. He tried to hide his surprise.

"Hello," she said. "Do you mind if I sit down?"

"Um…no. Sure." What else *could* he say? She sat down and rested her handbag on her lap. Angus hoped he wasn't about to be yelled at again.

"I want to apologise for the other day," she said, staring straight ahead. "When you and your friend came into my yard. It was unkind of me to scream at you like that."

"Um…that's okay."

"No, it isn't." She turned to him. "I haven't been feeling the best lately, but that's no excuse."

Angus wasn't sure what to say.

"I'm not really an evil, old witch," she continued, with a hint of a smile. "I just act like one sometimes."

Angus smiled back. He understood. It wasn't unheard of for *him* to act terribly on occasion.

She looked at Ben, now biting into an apple. "You're good with him, you know." How did she know? Angus remembered the twitching curtains. Had Mrs Screen been watching him with Ben?

She reached into her handbag and brought out a blue

velvet pouch. Tipping it up, five or six glass marbles dropped into her hand. They glinted and shone in the sun. Ben stopped chewing his apple to look.

"Lovely, aren't they?" said Mrs Screen, gently wiggling her fingers so that the marbles moved and the light danced through them. Some were emerald green, others sapphire blue. One large one was deep yellow right in the center. Ben dropped his apple in Angus's lap, got up from the bench, and stood in front of Mrs Screen.

"You can touch them if you like," she said.

Ben looked at Angus.

"Go ahead," he said.

Ben paused for a second, then reached out and ran a finger over the large yellow one.

"Ah, good choice. That's my Queenie. She's a cat's eye," said Mrs Screen. "Hold her and see how heavy she." Ben picked up the cat's eye and smiled.

Mrs Screen told Ben all about each marble, in turn. What it was called and the name for its size. Of course, he didn't say anything, and it was impossible to know if he was really listening, but he did seem to like the marbles. He was still staring at them as Mrs Screen put them back into the velvet bag.

"I must get on now," she said, getting up. "Janet will

be organising a search party if I don't get home soon." She smiled. "Lovely chatting with you…?"

"Angus. Angus Adams."

"Well, Angus Adams, if you still want to come and film your movie in my scary yard, then by all means do so. Good day to you, now." She walked off up the path. It was a quarter to five, time to take Ben back to Mr Jackson.

He was standing out in front of the center with another man whose shirt read "Affordable Glazing". They were staring at the doors. Or at least, what was left of them. They were completely smashed. Shattered glass lay all over the entranceway and on the floor inside. Angus pulled Ben back.

Mr Jackson set the glazier to work. "I found this thrown through the door," he said to Angus, holding up a brick. "With this wrapped around it." It was a note that read,

"Leave My Tree Alone Or You'll be Sorry!"

8 WIERDNESS & UNDEAD THINGS

"**A**re you sure this is going to work?" asked the big zombie, aka Hamish. He held the sheet while Angus clamped it to the curtain rod in his bedroom.

"Yes, I'm sure." Since a green screen does not, in fact, have to be green, they'd made their own from an old pink sheet Angus's mother had supplied. Of course, it wasn't as good as a proper green screen on a stand and everything, but you know, you have to work with what you've got.

"Bodhi, is the camera ready? It's hot in this costume." Hamish looked at his watch.

"Just about," said Bodhi, making a final adjustment to the tripod.

"And we can't take too long with this," he added. "Mum's picking me up at four-fifteen. She's enrolled me in Highland dancing. Can you believe it?"

"No," said Angus. "I cannot believe it. You? Highland dancing? I'm afraid I'm going to need video evidence. I'll talk to your mother about putting something on YouTube, shall I?"

"Don't you dare."

"Hang on a minute," said Bodhi. "The battery's just died. Wait while I plug the camera into the wall."

She hunted around for the lead. "Hurry up, will you,' said Angus. "I have to be at the center by four-thirty to watch Ben."

Hamish shook his head. "I can't get over old Mrs Screen chucking a brick through the door like that. And then sitting and chatting with you at the park. I mean, is that weird or what?"

"Yeah," said Angus. "The whole thing is really strange." He tried to imagine Mrs Screen sneaking about with a brick in her handbag, being careful not to crush her marbles, and then taking it out and hurling it at the doors.

"Personally, I think those marbles fell out of her head," said Hamish.

"Is Mr Jackson reporting it to the police?" said Bodhi, now back behind the camera.

"No, he's being weird, too," said Angus. He'd heard Mr Jackson talking with the center director. The director had wanted to go the police. Mr Jackson had talked him out of it, saying the glazier was a friend of his who owed him a favour, and was fixing the door for free. No harm done. No need for the police.

'Okay, we're ready," said Bodhi.

"LIAM!" called Angus. A small, but still hideous, undead thing with razor sharp teeth ran into the room. Bodhi came out from behind the camera and hugged him.

"You know, you're the cutest little zombie there ever was," she said. "Okay, now remember, you two, you're being chased by giant lizards that want to rip your heads off, tear your guts out and stomp through them, that kind of thing. Okay?"

"Sure," said Hamish. "Sounds fun."

***

Angus pushed Ben on the swing. It was once again busy at the park so he didn't hear Mrs Screen until she was at his shoulder.

"Good afternoon, Angus," she said.

Ben squealed with joy, leapt from the swing while it was still high in the air, and promptly fell face first into the sand. He jumped up again just as quickly, ignored their concern over his wellbeing and pointed urgently at Mrs Screen's handbag.

She laughed. "I take it you'd like to see my marbles again?"

Ben nodded enthusiastically, then actually took her by the hand and led her over to the bench. Mrs Screen took out the marbles and again explained each one to Ben, letting him touch them. He held them up to the sun, one by one, and smiled at the way the light danced inside them.

Angus watched on, waiting for the right moment. "Mrs Screen, can I please ask you something?"

She looked at him. "Yes, Angus. What would you like to ask?"

"Well, the thing is, I know you don't want your tree cut down, but, I mean…the center—"

"I don't want to talk about the tree." Her face clouded and she looked back at Ben lining up the marbles in a neat row at her feet. It was a long moment before she spoke.

"We had a tyre swing attached to that tree. When our daughter was a little girl it was her favourite thing. I'd spend hours and hours pushing her on it. She'd laugh and shout for me to push higher." She smiled. "When she was older she'd climb up and sit in the branches for entire afternoons, reading books or just singing to herself. That tree was her special place."

According to Finn, Mrs Screen's daughter had died at the house. Angus wasn't sure what to say, so he said nothing. Suddenly, Mrs Screen wrinkled up her face, closed her eyes, and put a hand to her stomach.

"Mrs Screen, are you okay?"

She opened her eyes. "I haven't been the best lately. Just an awful tummy bug that won't let go." She looked down at Ben. "Sorry, dear, but I need to go home now."

Ben picked up the marbles and gave them back to her, silently, as always. He watched solemnly as she put them into the velvet pouch.

After she'd gone Angus found a blue cat's eye under the bench. Mrs Screen must have missed it. He put it in his pocket to return to her later and glanced up at Scream House.

The wind blew the trees so that one moment the top window was revealed and in the next it was hidden. The hairs on the back of his neck stood up. It was like the house was winking obscenely at him.

9 DEATH ROW

Trumpet-Butt strode between the desks, pausing occasionally to peer over a shoulder. "Get a move on. By now you should all be making the finishing touches."

They were creating their own etchings for art class, which was actually a pretty cool thing. Angus looked down at his 6x9 zinc plate. Using the etching needle, he carefully drew the star on Captain America's shield. Done. He glanced at Hamish, who grinned and held up his Minecraft pig. Not bad.

"Once you have completed your design you will bring your plate, in an orderly fashion, to the front of the room and place it carefully into one of these white tubs."

Angus carried his etching to the front.

"Overnight, I shall put them through the acid bath to remove the excess 'ground', a task too dangerous for you simpletons. Tomorrow you will polish your plate."

Angus laid his plate carefully into a tub. Turning back to his desk he couldn't help looking at Mr Beuglehole. Why did he have to insult them at every opportunity?

"What's that look for, Adams?"

"Nothing, Sir." Angus put his head down and quickened his step but it did him no good.

"Adams, the art cupboard has been left in a terrible state by your previous teacher. You will tidy it during first break, thank you."

So, at first break, when everyone else was outside eating their lunch, Angus found himself buried in the art cupboard, organising the paints, pencils, and markers. On the bottom shelf were some bottles with poison warnings. Thinking that dangerous stuff should be on the top shelf where younger kids couldn't reach, he decided to move them. He read one of the labels. Acetonitrile.

He'd not heard of it before but the warning label declared in bright red letters:

"CONVERTS TO ARSENIC IF SWALLOWED - SEEK MEDICAL ASSISTANCE IMMEDIATELY"

Yikes. Angus had read enough mystery novels to know that arsenic kills people. These definitely needed to be on the top shelf. He was busy lifting them up when Mr Beuglehole appeared.

"What are you doing, Adams? Leave those where they are. I asked you to tidy the cupboard, not reorganise it."

"It's just that, well…I thought this stuff looked pretty dangerous, Sir."

"Don't answer back. And if you must know, I'll be using that for the etchings tonight and have no wish to have to lug it all down from up there."

"Yes, Sir."

Eventually, Angus finished with the cupboard and made it outside in time for the bell to ring and to have to go straight back inside. Fortunately, they were having Physical Education (PE) next. Unfortunately, Mr Beuglehole announced that the PE teacher was off sick, so he would be taking the class instead.

Great. Not.

Well, it was still PE. Surely even Trumpet-Butt couldn't ruin PE? Right?

Wrong.

The class headed to the oval, Hamish walked with Angus. "Watch out or he'll have you searching for four-leafed clovers at lunch time," he whispered.

"Yeah, wait for it."

When they arrived, Trumpet-Butt addressed the group. "Today we'll be covering the basics of Rugby League football. Evans and Pritchard, go and get the tub of balls and cones from the equipment shed."

Ruby League – awesome. This term, PE was focused on various codes of football and so far they'd covered soccer, American Grid Iron, and Australian Rules.

"Quiet 5/6A!" Everyone zipped their lips and looked to Trumpet-Butt. "We are being joined today by 5/6C. I expect you all to demonstrate exemplary behaviour."

Down the hill toward them trooped 5/6C. Bodhi waved at Angus and Hamish. Cool, a PE lesson with Bodhi, although no doubt she'd outshine the lot of them in Rugby as with everything else. At the back of the pack loped Rapata Takani. Not so cool. He gave Angus the evil eye.

They played Bull-Rush as a warm-up activity. Three

people were named as taggers, including Hamish. In Bull-Rush, the taggers each hold a ball and try to tag others while everyone rushes from one side of the playing area to the other. Those tagged must then pick up a ball and become a tagger for the next rush. The whistle blew and Angus charged. He dodged the grinning Hamish easily and made it to the other side safely. Bodhi was there ahead of him, of course.

There were now six taggers. At the whistle Angus took off. Two taggers came straight at him. He prepared to weave, then realised they were looking past him. He glanced over his shoulder. Rapata Takani was on his heels. He was always surprised by how quickly Rapata could move when he chose to. Rapata must also have realised the taggers had him lined up (and why wouldn't they? He was an easy target). He shoved Angus in the back and sent him flying straight into them. All three landed hard and Rapata loped past to the other side.

Angus picked himself up and offered a hand to the other two. He looked at Mr Beuglehole to see if he would intervene, but he wasn't looking, suddenly fascinated with his wristwatch.

After the warm-up (Bodhi was the last to be tagged and declared the winner) they moved onto an attacking drill known as Treasure Hunt. Balls and cones were placed in the center of the field as treasure, and four people were nominated as guards. Everyone else had to try to steal some treasure without being tagged. Not fifteen seconds passed before Rapata stuck his foot out and tripped Angus, sending him sprawling. He got up, determined not to react. Instead, he concentrated on making sure he knew where the giant was at all times, and keeping several bodies between the two of them. It seemed to be working. Until…

"Now we will move on to defence via some basic, front-on tackle practice," Trumpet-Butt said. "You will form pairs. One of you will be the ball carrier, the other the tackler. Form your pairs, please."

Hamish rushed to Angus. Bodhi paired up with a girl from her class. "Carriers, line up opposite your tackler," said Trumpet-Butt. Everyone lined up. "No, no, this won't do." Trumpet-Butt was looking at Rapata and his partner, Mitch Bobbit, known by most as Mitch *Hobbit* because of his short stature. He was probably the tiniest kid in their year. Next to Rapata, he did, in fact, look like a hobbit.

"Bobbit, we'll need to swap you with someone. Let's see…" Trumpet-Butt moved his eyes along the pairs.

Angus looked at his feet. *Don't choose me, don't choose me, please, heaven above, don't choose me!*

"Adams, swap with Bobbit." Angus looked at Hamish and swallowed. "Now, Adams. We haven't got all day."

With nothing for it, Angus walked toward Rapata like a prisoner sentenced to death. He didn't make eye contact. He glanced instead at Bobbit, who looked like he'd just received a life-saving call from the governor.

"Yes, that's much better. Takani, you be the tackler," said Trumpet-Butt. "Now, everyone, when I blow the whistle, you will move toward your partner. The tackler must perform a front-on tackle. Carriers, remember to keep moving. You don't want to give your tackler the advantage of momentum. If you fall, remember to roll safely away to the side."

Angus held the ball with two hands and faced Rapata. The whistle blew. Angus and Rapata moved toward each other. Rapata was a head taller than him so his own head was likely to make contact with Rapata's chest. *It's okay, just get tackled and if you have to, roll away to the side.* He braced himself for impact.

Smack!

Rapata wrapped him in a vice-like grip – there would

be no rolling to the side, just crushing to death. The ground rushed up. Angus dropped the ball and instinctively put his hands out. The weight of a mini-bus flopped on top of him as he hit the ground. An agonising pain shot through his left wrist.

Rapata rolled off. On the ground, Angus choked out a cry. The pain was unmistakable. "Sir, I think my wrist is broken."

Mr Beuglehole stood over him.

"You didn't roll safely away to the side, Adams."

10 THE BRICK THROWER

“**Y**es, a hairline fracture, I’m afraid.” The doctor tapped at the x-ray with a neatly manicured finger. “Not to worry, we’ll whack a plaster cast on and you’ll be as good as new in no time.”

Angus looked at his mother. She shrugged. “At least it’s not your writing hand.”

True. Okay, a broken wrist. Not so bad. Tomorrow, everyone at school would crowd around him and line up to write cool things on his cast. Kids who hadn’t been there when it happened would want to hear the whole story in a blow-by-blow account. For some weird reason a broken bone was a badge of honour at school. It made you just a little bit special.

"How long will I need to wear the cast for?"

"Six weeks should do it," said the doctor.

Six weeks. Cool.

"Of course, you can't get it wet. You'll need to put a plastic bag over it to shower. And, needless to say, no swimming."

Wait. *No swimming for six weeks?* He looked at his mother again. "But Ryan's pool party is in a couple of weeks. Can't I just put a bag over it?"

"No," his mother and the doctor said, together.

"Okay, well, I've seen other kids wearing those strap-on cast things that they can take on and off. Can't I have one of those instead of the plaster?"

The doctor fielded this one. "Those are used mostly for compression fractures. Unfortunately, yours is a bit more serious than that. Don't worry, the time will fly by."

Yeah, right.

***

With his arm in a sling and the plaster cast setting

nicely, Angus got out of his mother's car and said he'd see her at home. He was due to mind Ben and couldn't see that a little thing such as a fractured wrist should stop him. His mother wasn't so sure but agreed so long as Angus promised not to do anything stupid. He looked in through the car window. "So, skate-boarding's out then?"

He was a few minutes early. Mr Jackson hadn't arrived so he thought he'd cross the field to Scream House and return Mrs Screen's marble. He set off listening to some kids in a nearby backyard arguing over whose turn it was on the trampoline.

As he walked, his eyes were drawn up to the old house. Well, what he could see of it through the trees. It glared down at him, broodingly. Angus suddenly felt weird in his stomach. And the closer he came, the worse the feeling was. *Don't be an idiot. It's just an old house. Nothing to be scared of. Nothing sinister.* He blamed Finn for this. Finn and his stupid stories about the place being haunted. It wasn't haunted. Just old and run-down. Of course, the sad story of Mrs Screen's daughter dying there didn't help.

Everything was eerily quiet as he approached the gate. The arguing kids had disappeared. It was the same

maybe this whole strange business could be cleared up.

With his good hand he pushed branches and foliage out of the way (if he wasn't careful he'd lose an eye), while trying to protect his fractured wrist. It was difficult to follow the sounds of the person ahead due to the racket he was making himself. Underfoot, the crunching of dried leaves and twigs seemed deafening.

"Arghhh!" His foot snagged a tree root and down he went. A sharp pain shot through his damaged wrist. He cried out again.

"Angus? Is that you? Are you alright? What's going on?" The housekeeper, Janet, appeared. She helped him up. "I heard breaking glass and here you are face down in the garden. Goodness, what have you done to yourself?" she asked, looking at his cast and sling.

"It's the patio door." Angus cradled his poor arm. "Someone's thrown a brick through it. I was trying to chase them to see who it was."

"The patio door? Show me." She seemed to forget about his arm as she led him to a narrow path that ran along the side of the house to the rear patio.

"Oh, my Lord! Watch out for the glass." She slid what was left of the door open and carefully made her way in. She unwrapped the paper from the brick and studied it.

"One way or another the tree is going," she read. She put the brick down and brought her hands to her face. "This has to stop. Can't that man leave this poor woman alone?"

"It's not Mr Jackson." There was no way Mr Jackson would do this.

"I'm afraid I can't be so certain," said Janet. She walked back out to where Angus stood on the patio, climbed up on one of the old chairs, and peered towards the community center. "Yes, his car's there." She turned back to Angus. "What were *you* doing here, anyway?"

"Returning Mrs Screen's marble," he said quickly, and pulled it out of his pocket to show her. "She left it at the playground the other day." With unease, he realised that Janet might think *he'd* thrown the brick. "It wasn't me."

She gave a small laugh. "If it was, I would think you'd have left immediately, not come charging through the yard making such a ruckus. But whoever it was will be gone now. Still, they must have had a terrible fright when you appeared from nowhere and started chasing them." She looked at the marble in his hand. "Did you say Mrs Screen left that at the park? When was she at the park?" So Angus told her about the playground, Ben, Mrs Screen, and the marbles.

Janet stared out into the garden but remained silent.

"Er, Janet? Do you mind if I ask something?" She didn't answer so he plunged in. "Is it true that Mrs Screen's daughter died here?"

Her head snapped around. "No, she died in a car accident. Why do you ask?"

"Oh, well, it's nothing really. Just some dumb talk at school that this house is…well, that it's…haunted. By the ghost of Mrs Screen's daughter." He expected Janet to laugh at this but instead she went back to staring at the bushes for a long moment.

"Oh there are ghosts alright," she said finally. Then, oddly, she turned and walked away.

***

Since falling on it again, the pain in Angus's wrist was excruciating. He did his best at the playground with Ben (there was no sign of Mrs Screen today) but the pain forced him to take Ben back early. Concerned, Mr Jackson dropped him home. "You might want to get that looked at again, mate. See how you feel tomorrow, but the soccer clinic's on again if you're able to help out."

An hour later he was back at the hospital getting a

new plaster cast. His mother wasn't thrilled. "Honestly, Angus, five minutes after I tell you to be careful, you fall on it?"

"Sorry."

She sighed. "My fault for not insisting you stay home."

It was a different doctor. This one was a lady with bright red hair and a spider tattoo on her neck. As she applied the plaster she told his mother he'd need to stay home from school the next day while the cast set hard. But when Angus asked, she did agree that he should be okay to attend the soccer clinic after school as long he wasn't doing any running around.

At home later, the broken wrist proved to have some advantage as he wasn't expected to help with dinner. Instead, he tried to Skype first Hamish, then Bodhi, to fill them in on the latest brick-throwing incident and tell them he wouldn't be at school tomorrow. Frustratingly, he couldn't get hold of either of them.

The frustration continued the next day. In the morning he said goodbye to Liam, still the picture of misery, watched some cartoons on TV, then tried to finish his current Lego project (not Star Wars but the totally cool DeLorean, the car from the *Back to the*

Future movies) but it proved impossible with only one arm. His mother was working from home in the study and therefore no help in relieving his boredom. He couldn't even finish the last Harry Potter novel since he couldn't hold it and turn the pages at the same time. In the end, he settled for watching all three *Back to the Future* DVDs from start to finish, and was left wondering why no one had yet invented a real hoverboard.

It was a relief when late afternoon finally crawled around and it was time to walk to the soccer clinic.

At the center, the kids took one look at his arm and demanded to hear exactly how it had happened. The little kids especially oohed and ahhed in all the right places, except Ben, who just hugged his leg and said nothing.

"We missed you at school today," said Hamish. "Especially Trumpet-Butt. He had to pick on Perry instead, and I don't think he enjoys it as much."

Bodhi examined the cast. "This is a bummer. I was going to ask if you two would like to come to the beach with me tomorrow. But I guess there's no swimming for you, right?"

"Hamish can go," said Angus, trying not to feel

jealous of everyone whose arm wasn't in a plaster cast."

Before Hamish could answer, Mr Jackson spoke. "Actually, guys, I'm taking Ben to Robotronica in the city, tomorrow. If your parents say it's okay, I thought the three of you might like to join us?"

Robotronica? Awesome. Mrs Nesbit had mentioned it a couple of weeks ago. It was a big interactive showcase of robots and future robotic technologies put on by one of the universities.

"Yes, please," said Angus.

"I'd love to," said Hamish, "that is, if the heli—I mean my mother, will let me." While Hamish often called his mother 'The Helicopter' due to her excessive hovering, he tried to avoid it in front of other adults. Bodhi, who wasn't into robotics the way the boys were, said thanks but she'd stick with the beach.

"Okay then," said Mr Jackson. "All sorted." He turned to the rest of the group. "Righto, let's get started. Pair up for some passing practice, everyone."

The clinic finished early as Mr Jackson had an appointment to go to. Angus told the other two about Mrs Screen's door while they packed up.

"Wow," said Hamish, "and you caught a glimpse of whoever did it?"

"Barely."

"Well, what exactly did you see? A face?"

"Just a blur of the back of a head, and maybe an arm. That's it. Anyway, her tree still has the paint on it. Since we're done here do you think we should go over and offer to clean it off?

"Good idea," said Bodhi. "And maybe we could have a look around the yard. You know, to work out where we want to shoot the zombie scene. We still can, right?"

"No one said we can't," said Angus.

The three of them set off across the field, the gentle breeze feeling good against Angus's hot, sweaty face. Oddly, it dropped away to nothing as they neared the house.

At the gate, all three of them looked up at it. Bodhi bit her lip. "It is so strange, isn't it? I mean, bricks through doors, nasty spray-painted messages, everyone denying they've any involvement. I don't know what to make of it."

"I still think the old lady's doing it herself," whispered Hamish, as they entered the yard.

Angus couldn't imagine it. Mrs Screen had yelled at them in her garden that day, and she was capable of getting angry and upset, but throwing a brick through her own door? *Really?*

They looked at the tree that was causing all of the problems.

"Let's go up to the house," said Angus.

But before they could move, someone stepped out from the bushes and onto the path.

12 A NASTY SURPRISE

"**H**ello," said Janet, looking surprised. Angus quickly explained how they'd come to wash the paint from the tree.

"If you could please give us some soapy water and cloths we'll get started," said Angus.

Janet said that was a lovely offer and turned to get the water.

"Is Mrs Screen here?" Angus wanted to tell her that he'd had nothing to do with the brick, but Janet said she'd had her afternoon medication and was taking a nap.

Once they had cleaning gear, Janet left them alone and they got on with scrubbing the big ironbark, Angus doing the best he could with only one arm. The soap and water mixed with the paint to make the letters blurry, then unrecognisable as thick rivulets of reddish water ran down the trunk.

"It looks like the tree is bleeding," said Bodhi.

"No, it's crying." The three of them jumped. It was Mrs Screen. She walked up to the tree and rested her palm against it. "Poor old thing."

"Sorry, Mrs Screen, we didn't mean to wake you," said Angus.

"You didn't wake me. I wasn't really sleeping. Janet can be a bit too bossy for her own good. Sometimes it's easier to pretend." She continued staring at the tree.

Angus looked at Bodhi and Hamish. "Mrs Screen, these are my friends. You've kind of met Hamish already."

"Oh, yes, the day I was the screaming, evil, witch." Taking her hand from the tree she turned to them. "Oh dear, what happened to your arm?"

Angus gave her a brief run down.

"We'll have to work the broken arm into the movie, somehow," said Bodhi.

Mrs Screen waved at the yard. "Why don't you go on and make your movie now? For what it's worth, the yard is all yours. And, I agree, it is a pretty spooky old place. Why don't I show you around a bit?"

She moved off the path and to the side of the house and the three kids followed. The video camera was, in fact, in Angus's backpack but he explained that they didn't have their costumes with them, or the whole cast (they'd need Liam). But still, they'd love to have a look around and work out where they might film.

He tried to bring up the subject of the patio door but Mrs Screen didn't want to talk about it. Instead, as they walked along the path she pointed out various trees and shrubs with exotic sounding names like Hong Kong Orchard Tree and Leopard Tree.

Her grandfather had built the house in 1901, she said. He was a businessman and a local government councillor.

"Oh, the parties that were held here. My brother and I would hide on the veranda long past our bedtime and peek at the party-goers. The war had ended and people were having fun again. Glamorous ladies in beautiful gowns, men in bowties, all of them laughing, chattering, and dancing." She stopped to point through some trees. "Just in there you can see what's left of the rotunda where Grandfather had the musicians play." She gazed around. "He'd be disappointed to see the place now."

"It must have been very grand," said Bodhi.

"It was," said Mrs Screen. "I admit I've let things go. Since my daughter died, there hasn't been any point. There's no one to enjoy it anymore."

They kept walking and came to a small clearing. In the middle was a mould-covered wishing well. Mrs Screen explained it wasn't a real well and had only been for show. They all peered over its low wall to the dirt bottom. Hamish became excited and thought it might be a good idea if one of the zombies tipped Angus down the well. Angus thought it would work better if it was he who did the tipping and a zombie went down the well.

"What's that over there?" Bodhi pointed at something near the fence. Among the long grass was what looked like a ring of concrete toadstools sprouting up out of the ground. Mrs Screen confirmed that was exactly what they were.

"A local artist made them," she said. "When I was a little girl I would spend hours searching the garden for fairies, and Father thought I might like a special, magical place to sit and be close to them. Of course, my daughter, Jodie her name was, loved them, also." Faded though they were, it was clear that some of the toadstools had been pink; others, blue and yellow.

"What's this over the fence?" Hamish, not very interested in magic toadstool rings, had climbed onto the lower fence rail to peer over the top.

"Oh, that's the old bomb shelter," said Mrs Screen.

Bomb shelter? *Cool.*

Angus and Bodhi climbed up with Hamish. On the other side of the fence, a wooden trap door, or hatch, was set into the ground.

"Yes, we had everything from toadstools to bomb shelters," said Mrs Screen.

"What is a bomb shelter, exactly?" asked Hamish. "And why is it over the fence?"

Mrs Screen explained. "During the war people worried that enemy bombs would be dropped from planes so those who could afford it dug shelters into the ground. Just a small room, really. The idea was that a family could stay down there and be safe until the bombing stopped. Thank goodness we never had to use it. It's over the fence because part of the yard was sold long ago and this is where the new boundary went." She went on to explain that the neighbours had long since moved out.

"A bomb shelter would be awesome for the movie!" said Hamish, sounding hopeful. "Do you think we could use it for filming?"

"Oh, no, I don't think so. It hasn't been opened for years, and it might not be safe anymore. I don't even know where the key is."

"That's a pity," said Hamish, looking longingly at it. Before Angus climbed down from the fence he noticed that the large padlock on the hatch looked rather shiny and new. And if he wasn't mistaken, the long grass around the door had been recently trampled down.

Interesting.

***

At home, Angus used his good arm to unpack his backpack. At Scream House, they'd tried some camera angles and taken some test footage and now he wanted to download it and see how it looked. He pulled out his drink bottle, jacket, cap, a piece of yellow Lego, one of Liam's Pokémon cards, a rubber band…where was the camera? He thought back. The last thing he remembered doing with it was putting it on the veranda at Scream

House.

Running down the stairs, he called out, “Mum, I’ve got to go back to Mrs Screen’s place. I’ve left the camera there!”

Jogging wasn’t especially easy with a heavy cast. By the time he arrived, the late afternoon sun had slipped behind the house and it looked gloomier than ever. Long-fingered shadows stretched out across the garden. Angus had been to the house enough times now that he should have been less creeped out by it. But as he pushed the groaning gate open and made his way up, the trees seemed to reach for him. He had to admit that the creep factor was still pretty high.

Janet was on the veranda.

“Hi, Janet. Sorry, but I think I left my camera—”

The camera lay at Janet’s feet. What was left of it. It was smashed, as though someone in a heavy boot had stomped on it. The viewfinder was open and partly torn away from the camera body, which had caved in. The lens, too, was broken.

“What…? How did this happen?” This was bad. The camera belonged to his father.

Janet slowly shook her head. “She does strange things when she’s upset.”

"Huh? Who? Do you mean Mrs Screen did this?"

Janet picked up the broken camera and handed it to him. "I'm sorry."

13 ROBOTS & RESCUES

"So what did your dad say?" asked Hamish, in the back of Mr Jackson's car.

"I have to pay for a new camera." Angus's parents had not been happy. His mother said he'd behaved irresponsibly by ruining his plaster cast and then right on the heels of that he'd not taken proper care of his father's camera and now it was ruined.

"Buy a new one? Crikey, how are you going to do that?" Hamish was talking quietly, hoping Mr Jackson wouldn't hear over the radio. He was always a bit odd whenever anything to do with Mrs Screen was discussed.

"I'm going to earn the money delivering catalogues," whispered Angus.

"Really? What do you mean? Like K-Mart and supermarket catalogues? When are you going to do that?"

It had all been arranged the previous evening. Angus's father knew a guy who was a catalogue distributor. He was always looking for people to walk around and put them into mailboxes.

"Yeah. Weekends and afterschool, I guess." As jobs went, it wasn't a bad one, really. All he had to do was fold the catalogues and then deliver them to houses in his local area. The pay was pretty good. If he worked hard, he'd have enough money to buy a new camera in a couple of weeks. He might even keep the job after that, if his mother said he could. "Anyway, Bodhi's mother said we can use her camera in the meantime."

Hamish shook his head. "I'd just started to think Mrs Screen was okay. Like, nice, you know? When she was showing us around the place. But smashing your camera like that...Do you reckon she's crazy?"

"I don't think she did it." Angus looked out the window. They were on the Captain Cook Bridge. The city skyscrapers stretched upward over the Brisbane River, which sparkled in the sunshine.

Hamish looked surprised. "Then who did?"

Angus shook his head. "I don't know," he said. "But my gut is telling me that something really weird is going on in that house." Hamish looked at Angus's stomach as though it might suddenly start talking.

It didn't.

A few minutes later, Mr Jackson parked the car at the university hosting Robotronica and they all trooped up many stairs and into a huge hall. Ben held Mr Jackson's hand tightly and gazed about, wide-eyed.

"Wow," said Angus, doing plenty of wide-eyed gazing himself.

"Yeah, wow," echoed Hamish.

The place was alive with the strangest of sights and sounds. The enormous hall was filled with various displays and exhibits, all demonstrating new robotic technology of one form or another, with accompanying thrumming and buzzing noises and flashing, blinking, or strobing lights. There was already quite a crowd. Hundreds of people filled the spaces between and around the exhibits, staring, pointing, talking, and laughing.

"Okay," said Mr Jackson, over the noise, as he checked the information pamphlet. "What do you want to do first, boys?" There was a lot to choose from. Mr Jackson read out all the options. They could sign up to a free workshop where they'd get to make Lego robots and complete space missions (sounded cool), go bowling with robotic balls that they programmed first, play games like Sumo Robot Wars, or fly mini quadcopters through an obstacle course. There were also installations to see and demonstrations to watch. *Epic*.

Angus really wanted to see the Bigger Dipper Installation, a weird kinetic light sculpture, but Hamish argued that could wait until after they'd programmed a sumo robot. Scissors, paper, rock decided it, with Hamish's rock smashing Angus's scissors. Sumo robots it was.

"Okay, guys, I'll meet you back here in an hour," said Mr Jackson, checking his watch. "Try not to get lost." They assured him they wouldn't. Mr Jackson and Ben disappeared into the crowd for Robot Story Time.

Angus and Hamish took the stairs to the upper level in search of the Sumo Robot Wars room. It was a big place, with other corridors and doors leading from the main hall to even more displays and games.

Once in the correct room, they joined other kids on the floor and listened as the instructors showed them the robots, which were about the size of puppies, and explained how to use the iPads to drive them.

A pretty blonde girl sat on the other side of Hamish. She said hi to him. He said hi back and proceeded to blush a deep red right down to his own blonde roots.

There was time to practice driving the robots before the competition. As they clumsily manoeuvred them about, Angus heard the girl ask Hamish questions such as where he went to school, how much experience he'd had with robots, and commenting that he really seemed to know what he was doing so would he mind terribly helping her a bit?

Of course, Hamish said he didn't mind at all and showed her where she was going wrong. She smiled and thanked him. "You're welcome," said Hamish. "It gets easier the more you do it. I've driven these things heaps of times."

The girl chased her robot across the room.

Angus looked at him. "No, you haven't. What did you say that for?"

"I don't know. Crikey, it just came out. It's just…it's

just that it's always *you* getting all the attention for being smart and for once it's *me*." Then he furrowed his brow. "I didn't mean to lie, really."

Angus rolled his eyes as the girl, Crystal, skipped toward them. "Well, you better hope you do well in the Sumo War or you're going to look pretty stupid," he whispered.

Hamish's face crumpled. "I didn't think of that."

He needn't have worried. Whether it was skill or dumb luck, Angus wasn't sure, but Hamish proceeded to obliterate all his opponents, knocking them from the ring one by one, including Angus. "Well, I'm down to one arm at the moment," he said in his own defence.

At the end of the half-hour, Hamish received a winner's certificate and the gazing admiration of Crystal.

"Wow," she said, "you were awesome."

Hamish shrugged. "It was nothing," he said, but his smile stretched from ear to ear.

"Hey, you don't know which room the Deep Blue demonstration's in, do you? I really want to see that," said Crystal as they were leaving.

"Um…no, sorry."

"That's okay. Oh, here are my parents. I've got to go, but maybe I'll see you later?"

"Sure, bye," said Hamish. He and Angus watched the ponytail swing as she disappeared into the crowd.

They met up with Mr Jackson and Ben and together went to see a robotic arm that sorted marbles by size and colour. Angus had noticed it on the program and thought Ben might like it.

As Robotronica exhibits went, this was one of the less exciting. A large robotic arm sat on a table and plucked marbles, apparently randomly, from a glass container and then dropped them into one of five marble 'runs' (like curved slippery-dips for marbles) depending on the marble's size and colour. They watched as each marble hurtled down into a second container.

"This is lame," Hamish announced after a few minutes. "Let's go and do the 'Cars of the Future' thing."

But Ben didn't want to leave. He gripped the edge of the table, nearly tearing the fabric skirting off, and shook his head violently when Mr Jackson agreed they should move on. Mr Jackson gently tried to pull his arm away but Ben only made a loud howling noise and wouldn't stop. People began to stare. Mr Jackson got down on his knees so that he was eye level with his son.

He spoke gently: "Ben, listen to me. Let's watch the

marbles for two more minutes and then we'll go and have lunch in the cafeteria. You can have chocolate milk. Would you like that?"

Ben stopped howling and nodded his head.

"Two more minutes," repeated Mr Jackson, and asked Ben to hold up two fingers to show he understood. "You guys can go on. Meet us in the cafeteria if you like."

But neither Angus nor Hamish was hungry and instead went upstairs to the Cars of the Future workshop and programmed a mini car to navigate around a track. The workshop finished with races. Angus's car came second. Hamish's came last.

"Good thing Crystal's not here," Angus said, with a smile.

Hamish ignored him but as they left the room he pointed to a sign. "Look, Deep Blue. That's what she wanted to see. I wonder if she's found it yet."

From the upper railing they looked down at the crowd on the lower level. Angus spotted the ponytail. "There she is."

"Crystal!" called Hamish. But she didn't hear him, so Hamish bent down and stuck his head right through the railing.

"Crystal!" he yelled. That did it. She looked up and smiled. "Have you seen Deep Blue yet? It's up here!"

"Thanks! I'll come up," she called back.

"Okay," Angus said, "so what? Are we going to see this Deep Blue thing with her?"

Hamish didn't answer.

"Hamish?"

He still had his head stuck through the railing and mumbled something Angus didn't catch.

"What did you say? Stand up, for goodness sake, so I can hear you."

"I CAN'T, I'M STUCK!"

What?

Angus bent level with Hamish's head. "What do you mean 'stuck'?"

"I mean *stuck* as in *stuck*. I can't get my head out."

Angus laughed. He couldn't help it, even though Hamish looked upset; well, what Angus could see of his face through the railings, anyhow. Trust Hamish.

"Just twist your head around a bit and pull," said Angus.

"Do you think I haven't tried that? And it's not funny. Help me to get out before Crystal gets here."

Angus straightened up. "Okay, I'll try to pull on one

of the railings while you try to wriggle out." If he'd had two good arms he would have tried to pull the railings apart but with a broken wrist, that wasn't an option. He gripped the railing on the left of Hamish's head and pulled. "Okay, try now!" he grunted. Hamish twisted and turned his head as best he could but it was no use. Angus let go.

"Jeez, how'd you even get it through there in the first place?"

"Why do these things happen to me?" Hamish had gone red in the face, and looked like he might cry.

"Hey, you guys coming to Deep Blue?" It was Crystal. The smile slid from her face when Hamish failed to stand up.

"Um," said Angus. "We've got a bit of a problem."

"What?" She bent her head to try to see Hamish's face.

"Ah…well…Hamish is stuck. He can't get his head out."

She laughed. "You're kidding, right?"

"No," said Hamish. "I really am stuck."

Crystal said nothing for a moment, as though trying to decide if it was a joke or not. Finally, she said, "Gosh, you poor thing. Let me help you."

"Ah…no, it's okay," said Hamish, clearly dying of embarrassment to have her see him like this, head stuck, butt in the air. "You go on. Might see you later."

"If he ever gets his head out," said Angus.

"No. Look," said Crystal moving in closer. "Try pushing against the railing with your knee as you try to pull your head out. I'll pull from behind."

She clearly wasn't going away. Poor Hamish had no choice but to brace his knee against the railing and push against it while Crystal tugged at him from behind. Finally, he called out in exasperation:

"No, it's no use. I can't get it out!"

She let go.

"Oh, no." Hamish sounded weird.

"What?" asked Angus.

"Now my knee's stuck as well."

"Oh, for God's sake."

14 TRAPPED

It was true. Like his head, Hamish's knee was now firmly wedged between two of the railings. No one but Hamish could manage this.

"What's going on?" A couple of other girls, clearly friends with Crystal, had arrived on the scene. Crystal told them, in a serious tone, about Hamish's predicament. The girls broke out into peals of laughter.

"Oh, my God, this is totes hilarious!" said one.

"Too funny!" screamed the other, taking out her

phone. "I've just *got* to put this on Instagram!" She held the phone up and snapped a picture of poor, trapped Hamish.

"No, Sophie, don't. It's not funny," said Crystal. But the one called Sophie snapped away, regardless.

Angus felt bad for Hamish. It *was* a bit funny, true, but taking photos to shame him online was too much.

"Angus, help me," Hamish said, weakly, as he managed to pull his asthma inhaler from his pocket and take a few puffs. His asthma often became worse when he was stressed.

Angus wasn't sure what to do. He spotted Mr Jackson and Ben down below and called out to them. Mr Jackson had a go at pulling the railings apart, but even his strong arms couldn't budge them. "I'll get a maintenance staff member. Stay here," he said, and raced off.

Hamish sniffed. "Where does he think I'm going to go?"

There was now quite a crowd of onlookers. Hamish gave up all pretence of being brave and a couple of tears rolled down his cheek. Angus could do nothing but keep telling him they'd soon have him out. Thankfully, Crystal's parents had taken her and the giggling friends away. "Good luck," she'd said in farewell, looking sorry.

Mr Jackson returned with a couple of university maintenance workers. They rubbed Hamish's head and knee all over with olive oil from the cafeteria in the hope of making him slippery. All it did was make him smell like a salad.

The men stood back with hands on hips. "The railing will have to be cut away," said one of them, "and we don't have the right tools for that."

So they called in the fire brigade.

Two trucks turned up, complete with lights and sirens and a team of swarming firemen. As they worked to cut through the railing, a news crew, who'd been there anyway to cover Robotronica, began filming the 'rescue'.

The main attraction at Robotronica was now the boy with his head and knee stuck fast in the railing on the upper level.

The hall was noisier than ever with ear-splitting grinding as the railing was worked on. Angus stood back, watching. Who would have imagined the day would end like this? Someone grabbed his arm and he jumped. It was Mr Jackson.

"Angus, have you seen, Ben?" Looking around,

Angus realised he hadn't. With all the hoopla over Hamish he hadn't given Ben a thought.

"No, sorry."

"He was here just a minute ago," said Mr Jackson, looking all around, too. "It's so crowded in here. I can't believe I took my eyes off him."

This was all they needed.

"He can't be far away. I'll help you look," said Angus. They hunted all over the upper level, in all the smaller exhibit rooms, calling Ben's name, but he was nowhere to be found. Mr Jackson looked understandably flustered.

"Angus, could you please check again up here, including in the bathrooms? I'm going to search downstairs." He ran a hand through his hair. "I just hope he hasn't left the building."

The idea of Ben wandering around the city by himself was frightening. "Sure," said Angus.

He searched again. Leaving the boys' bathroom, he heard an announcement asking people to watch out for a little lost boy named Ben, describing the clothes he was wearing. Well, that was good. *Someone* will have seen him, surely. Convinced he wasn't anywhere upstairs, Angus headed to the bottom level.

The university's security team had now joined the hunt. A team of white-uniforms combed the hall and side rooms while another two stood at the wide front entrance to make sure Ben didn't leave the building, assuming he hadn't already. Angus knew Mr Jackson would have explained to them that Ben was a little different from most other kids his age.

A huge cheer came from the crowd on the upper level. *Had they found Ben?*

No. The cheer was for Hamish's head, now free. Unfortunately, his knee, jammed between two different railings, was still wedged in tightly. The screeching, grinding noise started again.

Things got crazier. A paramedic crew rushed in through the front doors. So that made a news crew, a fire crew, and now a paramedic crew. The place was knee-deep in crews. Well, if Hamish wanted attention, he was certainly getting it.

Of course it also meant more noise, more lights and sirens, more uniformed people dashing about. No wonder Ben had run away. He'd probably been completely freaked out by all the commotion.

Ten long minutes later, Hamish's knee was freed to an even louder cheer and a round of applause. While the firemen packed up their equipment, the paramedics made Hamish sit in a chair while they checked him over as a precaution. He was still using his puffer, and he had some nasty-looking red marks on his knee and his neck, just below the ears, but apart from that he was okay and declared good to go. The news reporter lady swooped in to ask him some questions.

But Ben was still missing.

The security team had combed the building. No one had seen him. Mr Jackson was frantic. The head security guy said it was time to call the police.

Angus thought hard. Where would a small, frightened boy hide? Not just *any* small frightened boy, but *Ben*. And then it came to him.

The marble room. *Of course!*

Mr Jackson was in deep conversation with the security team. Angus tried to politely interrupt.

"Excuse me? Mr Jackson?"

"Just a minute, Angus."

"Sorry, Mr Jackson, but I think I know where Ben might be hiding." That got all the adults' attention. "I bet he's in the marble room. You know, the marble sorting robot thing?"

"Sonny, we've thoroughly checked all the rooms

twice," said the beefy Head of Security.

"I looked in there myself, Angus," said Mr Jackson, "He's not there." His brow was creased with worry lines. The adults went back to their discussion. Apparently the police were due any minute.

Of course the marble room had been checked. But the thing was, no one here really understood about Ben and marbles. Not the way Angus did.

He went back to the room.

15 THE MARBLE ROOM

"**B**en? Ben, are you in here?"

Apart from the robot on the table, there was no one else here. The robot ignored Angus and continued to sort its marbles as though everything was just fine. *Brrrrr, clunk!* A marble rolled down its run and dropped into a jar. *Brrrr, clunk!...brrrr, clunk!* In the absence of other noise, the sound was rhythmic and soothing.

Angus lifted up the fabric skirting attached to the table and bent his head. It was dark under there, but he could just make out some packing boxes. *Brrrr, clunk!*

"Ben?" he said, quietly. Getting down on all fours, he crawled under the table, the fabric skirting falling into place behind him. Now it was *really* dark. As his eyes adjusted, he crawled around to search behind each box. "Ben, it's just me, Angus. It's okay to come out now."

Nothing.

Ben wasn't behind any of the boxes. Angus sank to his bottom and leaned against one, listening to the *brrrrr, clunks* in the near-darkness. "Where are you, Ben?"

The box moved.

Angus jumped and turned to look at it. It sat perfectly still, but it had *definitely* moved. And boxes don't generally move about by themselves. Unless, you know, there's *someone inside them!*

"Ben?" Angus lifted the cardboard flaps of the box. In the gloom he could just make out a pair of large, brown eyes staring back at him. He sighed with relief. "Come on, mate. Your dad's really worried about you."

***

Back in the main hall, Mr Jackson held Ben in his arms, hugging him tight. This was just as well because at that moment the police arrived, followed by a hysterical

Mrs McLeod, who mistakenly assumed they were there for Hamish.

"Oh good Lord! The *police*? What's happened now? Hamish? Where's Hamish?" she said, rushing to a bewildered police officer and grabbing his arm. "My friend, Carol, said he's on Instagram, hanging by his head, about to fall to his death, where is he? WHERE'S MY BOY?"

"It's okay, Mum, I'm fine!" called Hamish from the second level. Crystal was beside him again and Angus hoped, for his sake, that Mrs McLeod wasn't about to do anything embarrassing.

"OH HAMISH, LAD! DON'T WORRY! MUMMY'S COMING!"

***

It was official. Catalogue delivery sucked.

Angus trudged up the hill, pulling his granny trolley of catalogues behind him. It was an actual granny trolley, lent to him by his Nanna, with one wonky wheel that caused the trolley to pull to the right. The day was hot and humid. His hair stuck to his forehead, his armpits were drenched, and inside the cast his arm itched with no possible way to scratch it. A new kind of hell.

It was bad enough that it had taken three hours of his

Sunday morning to sort and fold all the catalogues (even with his mother helping because of his arm) but once out on the street things had gotten worse. He'd been chased by a dog and a bee (not at the same time) and then verbally abused by a cranky old man shouting, "No junk mail, sonny! Can't you read?"

He shoved a bundle of catalogues into what felt like the four hundredth mailbox and pulled at the trolley. One more street to go. Once he'd earned enough money to buy a new video camera he'd be quitting, that was for sure.

He turned the corner and stopped in front of the first house. Just as he was about to push the catalogues into the mailbox he noticed a sign on it declaring, 'No Hawkers'. *What's a hawker? Am I a hawker?* he wondered. He scratched his head. Who would have thought catalogue delivery would be so problematic. Unsure of his 'hawker' status, Angus thought he better not leave any catalogues, just in case. He was about to move on when the door of the house opened.

And out came Janet.

Janet? Mrs Screen's housekeeper? But didn't she live with Mrs Screen?

"Angus? Hi." She had a handbag over her shoulder

and car keys in her hand. She'd been heading for one of the two cars parked in the driveway but now came toward him. "Catalogues? Got yourself a job then. Good for you." She spoke quickly and kept glancing at the house.

"Hi, Janet. Is this your place? I thought you lived with Mrs Screen?"

With a strange expression on her face, she glanced at the house again, jingling her keys. Was it his imagination or was she nervous?

"Ah, no – I mean, yes, I do live with Mrs Screen. I'm…just…ah…housesitting for a friend. Well, not housesitting exactly, more just keeping an eye on the place while my friend's away. Okay, then, lovely to see you, but I really must get going." She seemed to be trying to end the conversation as quickly as she could. She jumped into the car, started it, and began reversing down the driveway. Suddenly she stopped, leaned across, and rolled down the passenger side window.

"Um…listen…how's everything going down at the center? Mr Jackson must be furious about the broken doors, right?"

"Ah, well, not 'furious' exactly, more…"—Angus searched for the right word— "*concerned*, I guess."

Janet didn't look particularly happy with this answer. She pursed her lips, then tried to smile, but it didn't really work. "When are you kids coming back to film your movie? I'll be away in the city all day tomorrow but you're welcome, anyway. After school, if you like."

"Okay, thanks. Bye."

She gave a brief wave and drove off.

Angus carried on. He had to finish the street and get to the community center to mind Ben. Janet had acted a little strange but right now just about everyone was acting strange.

Ten minutes later he was almost done. He'd been up one side of the street, down the other, and was now directly across from where he'd started. With great relief, he shoved his last bundle into the final mailbox and pulled the empty trolley to the corner.

A door slammed behind him. Angus turned to see a man leaving the house that Janet had come from. His mouth fell open.

It was Mr Beuglehole.

16 LIAM'S PROBLEM

"Trumpet-Butt and Janet?" Hamish was pop-eyed. "You're kidding? *Our teacher*, Trumpet-Butt?" It was a three way Skype between Hamish, Bodhi, and Angus.

"Are there any other Trumpet-Butts?" said Angus.

"Are they living together then?" asked Bodhi.

"I don't know," said Angus. "All I know is that she seemed nervous when she saw me, she said she was just minding the place for a friend, and then she drove away fast. Ten minutes later Mr Beuglehole came out of the same house and drove away."

"Maybe they're boyfriend and girlfriend, or married even," said Bodhi.

Angus scratched his chin. "Then why would she lie about minding the place?"

"Maybe it's not a lie. Maybe they're both minding it? Are you sure he didn't see you?"

"I'm sure," said Angus. "I hid behind a tree and he didn't even look in my direction."

"Well, who cares, anyway?" said Hamish, impatiently, "What I want to know is have you seen Mrs Screen and has she explained what happened to the camera?"

Angus *had* seen Mrs Screen at the playground. This time she'd been there ahead of them, already seated on the bench. Ben had rushed to her, gave her a big hug, and then pulled at her handbag, wanting to see the marbles. While they were doing the marble thing, Angus eventually worked up the courage to ask about the broken camera.

"I didn't break your camera, love. Why on earth would I?" She seemed genuinely surprised, but before they could discuss it further she became unwell again and rushed off home, her hands across her stomach.

"Well, if Mrs Screen didn't smash the camera then the only other person who could have is Janet," said Bodhi.

Hamish threw his hands up. "But *why* would she?"

Angus sighed. "She wouldn't. Nothing makes any sense."

***

Angus sat on his bed and continued thinking about things. *Who* had smashed his camera? *Who* had spray-painted Mrs Screen's tree and broken her door? And had it been Mrs Screen who'd vandalised the community center? If it wasn't, then *who* was it and why were they doing these things?

He didn't yet have the answers but his stomach rumbled loudly, announcing itself hungry. Time to raid the fridge for a pre-dinner snack. Passing Liam's room he heard crying. He pushed the door open.

"Liam?"

He looked up from the bed, his tear-stained face screwed up in misery. "Go away, Angus."

Angus sat next to him. "Liam, please tell me what's wrong. And don't bother saying there's nothing wrong because I know there is." Liam remained silent. "Is it Rapata?"

Liam sniffed and then, very slowly, pulled up his t-shirt. Angus gasped. There was a huge purple bruise spread across Liam's rib cage. Angus clenched his fists.

"Who did this? Was it Rapata?"

"I can't talk about it!" Liam pulled his shirt down. "I can't Angus, I just can't."

"Then I'm telling Mum and Dad."

"NO! Angus, no, please don't tell them!" He sobbed loudly.

Angus put his good arm around Liam's shoulders. "Liam, you can tell me. Really you can. Someone's hurting you and I can make it stop."

"No, you can't. Rapata said he'd hurt you worse if I told, and…and… then he broke your arm! Oh, Angus it was my fault he broke your arm 'cause I said I was going to tell you!"

So there it was. Of course Rapata was behind it all.

"But tell me *what*, Liam? Tell me *what*?"

For a moment it seemed that Liam would clam up again, but then the wall crumbled and out it came. Rapata had been bullying Liam and two of his friends. Each day at school he forced them to hand over their lunches and pocket money or else he would beat them up, he said. When Liam refused, Rapata made good on his threat and punched him, leaving the nasty bruise on his ribs.

Angus was furious. Like all brothers, he and Liam often argued and, sure, sometimes he was annoying, but the thought of someone hurting Liam brought feelings of white hot rage. No wonder Liam had been so miserable. He was *terrified.* And it explained why he'd been both sick *and* hungry all the time. His brother was getting through each day at school with nothing to eat.

Liam continued to sob. "Angus, you can't do anything. You can't tell Rapata that you know, 'cause he'll hurt us even worse!"

Angus pulled a clean tissue from his pocket and gave it to him.

"No, he won't. I'll take care of it. Just leave Rapata to me."

17 BAD GUYS

The Darth Vader radio alarm clock burst into song. An overly chirpy number about a brand new day. Angus reached out his good hand and smacked it into silence, then pulled the covers over his head. He did *not* feel like facing a brand new day. It was a school day, and since Mr Beuglehole had arrived, school was not a very nice place to be.

There was one good thing. Liam's class was going on a farm excursion and would be out of school for the whole day. There would be no need to worry about him, today anyway.

Through the covers he heard the door open. "Come on, mate. Up you get, don't forget we're leaving early." Dad. Now he remembered. Mum was going with Liam on the excursion and he was getting a lift to school with Dad in the truck. His parents wouldn't let him ride his bike one-handed, saying he'd likely fall off and break the other arm, too. *Parents*. What could you do?

Forcing himself out of bed, he trudged downstairs. Thirty minutes and a bowl of cereal later, they climbed into the truck. It was early because Dad needed to stop at the police station. His father ran a bin-cleaning business and someone had been vandalising the wheelie bins of a couple of his elderly customers. Dad had offered to report it for them.

"Won't take long, mate," his father said over the engine, "I've already called them about it. They just want me to come in and sign something."

Angus didn't mind at all. Police stations were cool. The last time he'd been to one (okay, the *only* time) he, Hamish, and Bodhi had uncovered a car-stealing operation and had to give important statements to the police, who'd buzzed all over them and treated them like mini celebrities. Maybe they'd recognise him today.

They didn't.

Angus looked around while his father went to the counter. Last time he'd been too excited to take much in but now that he really looked, it was a little disappointing. There were a few chairs and a bench seat, some potted plants, and a table with magazines. People were working behind the counter, but most of them weren't even wearing uniforms, just ordinary clothes. It looked more like a doctor's waiting room than a police station.

He sat on a chair to wait and noticed a few 'WANTED' posters on the wall. Now *this* was more like it. *Bad guys!* From his seat he examined the faces. Maybe he would recognise someone and help catch a crook. He imagined himself jumping up and shouting that Bad Guy Number 3 was, in fact, the school lollipop man (he'd always looked suspicious), and the police insisting he, Angus, go with them, lights and sirens blaring, guns drawn, to help arrest the guy.

He studied the faces carefully. The first poster showed a woman who, if Angus squinted and turned his head to one side, looked a little like Lady Gaga. The second poster was of a couple in a grainy shot that looked like it had come from a security camera. The woman's face was partly turned away but it had caught the man front on. Dark hair, long dark beard, big nose. Definitely not the lollipop man. The next poster was a guy who looked *a lot* like Messi, the soccer player, and the last guy reminded Angus of Elmo, but apart from that he didn't recognise anyone. *Bummer*.

"All done, mate. Come on, or you'll be late," said Dad, tugging his arm.

"Dad, wait. Look at these pictures. Recognise anyone?"

His father gave them a quick glance. "No, mate, afraid not. You've been watching too much TV. Let's go."

***

The school bell rang as Angus darted through the gate and up the path to his classroom. He filed in with the other kids, thankful to have made it on time.

Mr Beuglehole, who was never very happy even on the best of days, was in a foul temper. He barked orders all morning and stomped up and down between the rows of desks, glaring at everyone. Hamish knocked over a container of pencils and muttered a soft 'crikey'. Mr Beuglehole pinned him with a death stare and said that if heard Hamish say ‘crikey’ one more time he’d feed him to a crocodile and he could join Steve Irwin in the afterlife.

It was a relief when the bell for first break rang. Once they’d finished their sandwiches, Angus and Hamish played handball until a particularly awesome ace from Angus flew past Hamish and rolled under the building. Their classroom was the temporary type, raised up on stumps. Neither of them wanted to be the one to crawl on hands and knees to retrieve the ball, but it was Hamish’s best one and he didn’t want to just leave it there. Scissors, paper, rock decided it and down Angus went.

It was gross. He crawled past a discarded rotten banana, a mouldy left shoe, and something green that stunk suspiciously like it may have been a tuna sandwich in a previous life. As he reached for the ball he heard a voice.

It was Mr Beuglehole. He was still in the classroom on the other side of the floorboards directly over his head.

“So has she signed it?...Yes! Well done. Where are you now?” He was clearly talking on the phone. “Good, good. Finally, after five years. Not long to go now…No, not until she's dead, you fool...Listen, I told you before I think you've made a mistake with the boy – he's trouble. Just be careful...God, I can't wait to be out of this dump."

The bell rang and Angus heard nothing further as he crawled out. What a weird conversation. Was Mr Beuglehole planning to leave soon? Well, that'd be good. *Not until she's dead?* Until *who's* dead? He stopped. Suddenly his knees felt weak. What if the person on the other end of the phone had been Janet? Now he felt sick. What if they'd been talking about Mrs Screen? *Not until she's dead.*

Angus didn't know what to do. Should he run to Mrs Screen right now and tell her what he'd heard? Should he confront Trumpet-Butt and demand to know what he'd been talking about? In the end, he decided he wouldn't do anything until he could discuss it with Hamish and Bodhi.

During class, one thing was certain. Whoever he'd been talking to and whatever it had been about, the phone call had much improved Mr Beuglehole's mood. His usual scowl had been replaced by a smug little smile, and instead of stomping up and down he positively strutted.

At lunch time Angus told Hamish and Bodhi what he'd overheard. "We should tell Mrs Screen, right?"

"Yes," said Hamish immediately. "Before they kill her. Why do they want to kill her?"

"I don't know, Angus," said Bodhi with a furrowed brow. "You can't be certain he was talking to Janet, and the whole conversation may have had nothing to do with Mrs Screen, let alone a murder plot."

"Because she's rich!" Hamish blurted out, eyes popping.

"What?" said Angus and Bodhi, together.

"They want to kill her so they can have all her money. It's obvious."

They discussed it some more without getting anywhere. Hamish was convinced Mrs Screen was in mortal danger while Bodhi insisted on being annoyingly logical and pointing out the lack of evidence. "And it would be awful if you told Mrs Screen and she fired Janet and then it turned out Janet was innocent," she added.

Angus went back to class still unsure what to do.

And then, mid-afternoon, something happened that changed everything.

They were doing drama; acting out scenes from a

novel set during the time of the first settlers. Being in such a good mood, Mr Beuglehole even joined in, covering his bald head with a thick, black wig and donning a long, matching beard.

“How do I look?” he said to the class.

Angus did a double take. In the beard and wig, Mr Beuglehole didn’t just look weird, he looked…*familiar.* And then it hit him. Angus nearly fell over.

There was no doubt about it.

Mr Beuglehole was the man in the ‘Wanted’ poster. The one who’d been with a woman. And the woman was Janet.

18 POISON

It took Angus every ounce of self-control to get through the school day without running from the room screaming. As drama class continued, he tried to process it all while still acting normal – he certainly didn't want Mr Beuglehole to know he was on to him. *So stop staring and close your mouth!*

Okay, so his new teacher was a criminal wanted by the police. His partner was Janet, Mrs Screen's housekeeper. He remembered the poster had stated they'd been on the run for seven years. So *were* they trying to kill Mrs Screen?

The poster had also said they were wanted for fraud, which Angus knew meant tricking people out of money. So, was Hamish correct in thinking they were after Mrs Screen's money? Did she even have any money? Sure, everyone said she was rich but if that were true then surely Scream House wouldn't be so run down. And how did any of this fit in with the community center and the vandalism? He was certain now that Janet had smashed his camera, but *why* had she done it and *why* had she tried to make him think it was Mrs Screen?

Only one thing was really clear in his mind. He had to tell Mrs Screen what he knew. Mrs McLeod was giving him a lift home so when the bell finally rang he babbled it all to Hamish on the walk to the car.

"Crikey," said Hamish. "Wanted by the police! Are you sure it's them? Shouldn't you go straight to the cops?"

"Yes, I'm sure. I'm going to see if Mrs Screen will come to the police station with me. I think I should tell her first. Janet will be in the city all day today, she said, so she won't be there. Wanna come?"

Mrs McLeod waved to them through the windscreen.

Hamish lowered his voice. "I can't. I've got to go to tutoring. And don't say anything in front of Mum. She's still freaked out about the whole 'getting my head stuck' thing and is hovering worse than usual. Who knows what she'll do if she hears *this* story."

So on the ride home, Angus said nothing about Mr Beuglehole or Janet. This wasn't difficult as Mrs McLeod insisted he eat one of her fresh-from-the-oven, and about-the-size-of-your-head blueberry muffins. So his mouth stayed full.

At his house, he climbed from the car, waved goodbye, and ran to his bike as soon as Mrs McLeod turned the corner. There was no time to waste. He wasn't supposed to ride with his broken arm but surely this counted as an emergency.

Pedalling flat-out, he was soon at Scream House. At the front gate he hesitated for a second and looked up. As usual, the house leered at him, unwelcoming and secretive. He wasn't frightened of it, exactly. It was just a house, after all. It was people you had to sometimes watch out for. People like Janet and Beuglehole.

With a deep breath, he went through the creaking gate, dumped his bike and helmet, and jogged to the front door.

He knocked loudly. "Mrs Screen? Are you there, Mrs Screen?" There was no answer so he made his way along the overgrown path to try the kitchen door.

Suddenly, a banging noise came from his left and something darted from the bushes. His heart leapt to his throat and he was about to scream before he realised it was only a cat. It scampered off down the path and left Angus with his heart pounding in his ears.

Curious as to what had caused the noise, he stepped off the path and pushed back the bush where the cat had come from him. To his surprise he saw what looked like a door. He pushed his way through, protecting his broken arm, and found himself standing in front of a garden shed. Being in such an overgrown part of the yard, he hadn't noticed it before. The door was swinging in the breeze and banging whenever it hit the shed wall.

Angus peered inside. He expected to see regular garden shed stuff like a lawnmower and maybe a rake and a few tools, but it contained only a table and shelves. The table had papers on it and he didn't generally like to snoop so didn't look at them too closely. Instead he looked at the shelves.

And gasped.

First, he noticed the red and green cans of spray paint

and thought immediately of the community center shed and Mrs Screen's tree. The second thing he noticed were some familiar bottles. Bottles with huge poison warning labels on them. The Acetonitrile from the art cupboard at school! The stuff that turns into arsenic if you drink it. Suddenly, an image of Mrs Screen clutching her stomach in pain popped into his head. Was she being poisoned?

Feeling he had every right to now snoop, Angus looked at the papers. The top one was headed "The Last Will and Testament of Elizabeth Screen", with 'COPY' stamped across the top. He quickly scanned the document. Mrs Screen was indeed leaving all her money to Janet. The date under the signature at the bottom was today.

Angus remembered Mr Beuglehole on the phone that morning. *So, has she signed it?...Yes, well done...no, not until she's dead.*

He hurried from the shed, pushing his way through the bushes to the path. He ran to the kitchen door and tried the handle. It was unlocked. He pushed the door and stuck his head in. "Mrs Screen? Mrs Screen, are you okay? It's me, Angus," he called. There was still no answer so he went through the kitchen and found himself in a wide hallway leading to a grand staircase.

"Mrs Screen, are you upstairs?" Silence. Should he go up? Suddenly, he remembered that Mr Jackson was at the community center. He'd know what to do. As he turned to go back through the kitchen, he heard something. Someone was calling out, faintly, from upstairs. It was more like a groan than a call.

He bounded up, two stairs at a time, yelling Mrs Screen's name.

"Angus? Angus, in here." He pushed open a door. Mrs Screen lay on her bed with one hand across her stomach. Her face was deathly pale and beads of perspiration dotted her forehead. She reached out the other hand to him. "Help me, Angus," she whispered. "My stomach hurts."

He went to her and took her hand. It felt hot and clammy. "I'll get help," he said. "Don't worry, I'll be back in a minute." He ran from the room, down the stairs, through the kitchen and into the yard, and then through the back gate. "Mr Jackson! Mr Jackson!" he screamed as he sprinted across the field. Thank goodness his car was in the carpark.

As Angus neared, Mr Jackson and Ben came out. "Angus, what is it? Are you okay?"

He stopped and tried to talk, puffing from the sprint. Ben hugged his leg. "It's Mrs Screen," he finally panted out. "She's very sick. You need to come quickly."

Mr Jackson scooped up Ben and ran with Angus back to Scream House. Angus had expected to have to direct Mr Jackson to the kitchen door but he didn't need it. Taking the lead, Mr Jackson ran straight to the door and inside. "She's upstairs," said Angus.

Still carrying Ben, Mr Jackson raced up the stairs and into the room with Angus close behind. He put Ben down and went to Mrs Screen. "Elizabeth, what's wrong?"

Elizabeth? Mrs Screen looked at him. "Oh, Bradley," she said.

Bradley? This was getting weirder.

Ben climbed onto the bed and cuddled into Mrs Screen. She smiled and stroked his hair. Now it was Mr Jackson's turn to look bewildered as, of course, he didn't know that Ben had been seeing Mrs Screen at the playground.

"What's wrong, Bradley, can't I cuddle my own grandson?"

GRANDSON?

19 *WHAT? REALLY?*

Angus couldn't contain his confusion. "I don't understand. Why are you calling Ben your grandson?"

Mrs Screen looked at him and then at Mr Jackson. "Will you tell him, or shall I?" But before anyone could tell him anything Mrs Screen gave a small cry of pain, screwing her face up tightly. Mr Jackson took out his phone and rang for an ambulance.

"They're coming," he said. With a sigh he sank into the chair by the bed and put his hands in his lap.

"Mrs Screen is Ben's grandmother," he said. "Her daughter, Jodie, was my wife."

Woah.

Okaaay…so Mrs Screen's *dead* daughter and Mr Jackson's *dead* wife were the same person. Wow.

But wait, it still didn't make sense. "I don't get it," said Angus. "Why do you two act like you're not even friends? If Mrs Screen is Ben's grandmother, why didn't they know each other when we first met at the playground?"

"So you made friends at the playground?" said Mr Jackson, now understanding. He looked at Angus. "Mrs Screen and I haven't spoken since Ben's mother died. She blames me for her daughter's death, Angus, and she's never forgiven me. She thinks I should have been here to take care of her daughter, not overseas in the army. And she's probably right."

"That's not true!" Mrs Screen struggled to sit up. "How can you say that, Bradley? It was *you* that wrote me that letter saying you blamed *me* for her death and that you'd make sure I had nothing to do with my grandchildren ever again!"

"*What?*" Mr Jackson stood up. "Elizabeth, I didn't write you any letter. It was *I* who received a letter from *you.*"

"It was Janet!" Angus blurted out. He'd worked it all out. "It was Janet who sent those letters to each of you – and it's still Janet!" In a rush he told them how Janet and Mr Beuglehole were wanted by the police, about the poison and spray-paint he'd just found in the garden shed (Mrs Screen said she'd never had a garden shed so Janet must have put it there herself), and about the copy of the will.

"She tricked you into re-writing your will and now they're trying to kill you so they can get the money! She's been giving you poison!"

Mrs Screen sank back onto the pillow, looking pale.

"Elizabeth, when did Janet begin working for you?" asked Mr Jackson.

"A few months before Jodie died, while you were away. She started with a gardener- fellow but he left soon after Jodie's accident."

"Do you have a photo of him?" asked Angus. He had a feeling about the gardener.

Mrs Screen told Angus to look in the bottom drawer. It didn't take him long to find the picture. It showed a younger Janet standing with a man on the veranda of Scream House.

"That's Mr Beuglehole," said Angus, handing the picture to Mr Jackson.

"It sure is," said Mr Jackson.

"Now it makes sense," said Mrs Screen. "Over the past few months I've been watching you, Bradley, with my little grandson, at the center. I can see a lot from upstairs here. It hurt so much to see Ben so close and...well, I'm getting older and I wanted another chance to know him. So I mentioned to Janet that I might try to make amends. Try to talk to you and see if we couldn't work things out. But before I could, this tree issue came up and then…and then the tree was vandalised and my door smashed, and I began to feel sicker and sicker each day. Oh, Bradley, Janet convinced me it was you doing all of those things because you hated me."

"But it was Janet," said Angus. "And probably Mr Beuglehole. They did everything, to your house and to the center, so that the two of you would hate each other. She was worried that if you made friends again, then she wouldn't get all the money. Is that right?"

Sirens could be heard coming up the street. "I think that's right, Angus," said Mrs Screen, weakly. "I thought Janet was my only friend in the world. I signed the new will this morning and she's taken it to the lawyers in the city. But thanks to you, love, she hasn't managed to kill me." She rubbed her stomach. "Not quite, anyway. And now I have my grandson at last." Through teary eyes she looked at the small boy, still cuddled into her. "Granny loves Ben," she said.

"Ben loves Granny," he whispered back.

***

The paramedics arrived while everyone was still recovering from the shock of Ben speaking for the first time in his life. After examining Mrs Screen, they carried her on a stretcher to the waiting ambulance. Angus showed them the bottles of poison in the shed and together with Mr Jackson told them what they suspected.

"You're lucky to have found her in time," said one of them. "And you should call the police right away." Mr Jackson rang them then and there on the veranda while Ben was upstairs, playing with marbles.

He hung up. "The police are coming right now. They want us to meet them out the front."

"Janet told me she was going to the city today but, well, I mean it's late afternoon now. What if she comes back before the police get here?" said Angus, looking up the street.

"Well, then I'll keep hold of her," said Mr Jackson.

But it wasn't necessary. When the police arrived there was still no sign of Janet. They listened to the story, took notes, asked lots of questions, and were very interested to see the garden shed with the poison. A police photographer arrived and the shed was taped off for photographs.

"We'll fingerprint everything in here," said a tall policeman. "If they are the wanted couple, then their real names are Thomas and Mary Slaughter. The house will be dusted for prints, too, so please remain outside." Mr Jackson said he'd have to fetch Ben from upstairs.

Angus waited out the front with the police. "We still need to put all the pieces together, of course, but on the face of it, mate, I'd say you've done a good job, here. Well done on recognising these two from the poster," the tall one said to Angus. But before he could reply, loud footsteps thumped through the house. "Ben! Ben where are you?"

Mr Jackson appeared at the door, his face white.

"Ben's gone," he said.

20 *KIDNAPPED?*

Mr Jackson and Angus weren't allowed back in the house while the police looked for Ben, so they began to search the yard since he might have gone out the kitchen door.

It was a big house and an even bigger yard, with many places for a small boy to hide. Together they pushed back bushes and shrubs, and were scratched all over as they called Ben's name. "He'll be here somewhere," said Mr Jackson and Angus could see he was trying hard to remain calm.

But Ben wasn't anywhere. More police came and the house and yard were thoroughly searched. Afternoon turned to evening and the search was widened to the surrounding streets. Mr Jackson was frantic.

On dark, the tall police officer dropped Angus home, although he didn't really want to go. He would have preferred to keep searching with everyone else. "Mate, there's nothing more you can do tonight. We appreciate everything you've done so far, now go and eat something and get some sleep," said the officer.

Angus's parents listened to the story in amazement. They turned on the evening news and there it was. Nothing about Mrs Screen and the poisoning, just about Ben being missing. An army of volunteers was being formed to help the police search surrounding bushland through the night. Angus's father went to join them, but he, too, wouldn't let Angus go. "Not through the night, mate. You've already got one broken arm."

To have to sit around and do nothing when little Ben was out there somewhere totally sucked. He forced down some of the dinner his mother put in front of him and then Skyped Hamish and Bodhi.

"I knew they were trying to kill her!" said Hamish. "Crikey, didn't I say so? So, has Trumpet-Butt been arrested yet?"

"Not as far as I know," said Angus. "Last I heard, the police were still looking for them both."

"So, Janet—I mean Mary, or whatever her real name is—didn't come back to the house after lodging the will in the city?" said Bodhi, looking thoughtful.

"No," said Angus, "and she won't go there now. Not with all the police cars in the street."

Bodhi scratched her head. "Don't you think it's odd that she didn't come back? I mean, wouldn't their plan have been to keep poisoning Mrs Screen until she died? Why wouldn't she have come back?"

Angus didn't have a good answer. With Ben going missing he hadn't had a chance to think everything through. After the call ended, he lay on his bed and thought some more.

Of course, it was possible Janet *had* returned to the house earlier and seen the police or even the ambulance and so took off again. Then something occurred to him that made his stomach roll over.

He sat up.

What if Janet had come home while he and Mr Jackson were at the house talking to Mrs Screen? She could easily have come in, crept up the stairs, and overheard them. What would she do once she realised her plan was ruined? Get away again fast? But what if she hadn't? What if she came up with a new plan and hid somewhere until the ambulance left?

What if Janet had taken Ben?

He stood up and began pacing. But *why*? Why would she take Ben? Well, maybe when she realised the plan was ruined, realised they wouldn't be getting all Mrs Screen's money the way they'd thought, maybe Janet decided to kidnap Ben and demand money to return him. That was what kidnappers did, wasn't it? Demand money?

He needed to tell the police.

He ran downstairs and blurted out the theory to his mother.

"Well, I guess it's possible," she said, "but Ben's run off before, hasn't he? I would think it's most likely that he's run off again this time. That Janet and Mr Beuglehole will be miles away from here by now."

"But, Mum, what if they're not?" Angus begged and pleaded until she finally agreed to try and tell the police. This proved difficult. She phoned the station and was told she was just one of many people calling in with supposed information about the missing boy. She couldn't make them understand that she wasn't just 'anyone', she was the mother of the boy who'd alerted the police to the whole situation in the first place. She was told someone would call back.

After more pleading from Angus, she called his father and told him what Angus suspected. He said he'd do his best to find the officer in charge and talk to him. A long forty-five minutes later, Dad called back.

"Mate, they agree it's possible that Janet took him but say they're already looking for her and that Beuglehole bloke. So far no one's demanded any money and the police know that Ben has run off before so they think he's most likely just hiding somewhere this time, too. Oh, by the way, Mr Jackson asked me to tell you that Mrs Screen is going to be okay, thanks to you. Now go to bed and get some sleep."

But sleep proved hard to get. Angus tossed and turned and kept waking from unpleasant dreams in which Mr Beuglehole was trying to make him drink poison. When morning finally came he raced downstairs to hear if Ben had been found. Dad was at the kitchen table, drinking tea and looking exhausted. His mother was cooking eggs. Ben had not been found and neither had Janet or Mr

Beuglehole. The search for Ben would continue that day.

"Well, I'm helping," said Angus.

"No, you're not," said his parents together.

"*What?* Why not?"

"Because you have a broken arm, the police need to be left alone to do their job, and you should be in school," said Mum.

He tried to argue, but it was pointless. He had to go to school.

***

The school yard was buzzing with the news that Mr Jackson's son was missing. Nearly everyone had seen it on television the evening before or else had heard about it. He was well liked and the whole school was alarmed and worried.

Mr Beuglehole, of course, wasn't there. A relieving teacher, Mrs Walters, took the class and announced that he was no longer at the school. Angus was sure he didn't imagine the entire class heaving one huge sigh of relief. Mrs Walters said she'd be taking the class in the interim until a permanent replacement for Mr Beuglehole could be found.

Perry took out his notebook and added 'interim' to his list of new words. Hamish said 'crikey' five times in the next fifteen minutes. He and Angus went to Robotics class at 9.30. Mrs Nesbit, the robotics teacher, was pleased to have them back. "How's the wrist, Angus?" she said. "I saw you delivering catalogues the other day. That can't have been easy with only one arm."

Angus felt uneasy all day. It wasn't just worry about Ben. There was something nagging at the back of his brain. Something obvious that he was missing, or had forgotten. It had something to do with Mrs Nesbit's comment about delivering catalogues.

"You told the police about the house, right?" said Bodhi, on the walk to the school gate that afternoon.

"What house?" said Angus. Then it hit him like a cream pie in the face. The house! The house where he'd seen both Janet and Mr Beuglehole when he’d been delivering catalogues. How could he have forgotten that?

21 *ANGUS GETS IT WRONG*

After school Angus rode, one-armed, straight to the community center, now the search headquarters since Scream House had been cordoned off for forensic work.

"Mr Jackson!" Angus ran into the building.

"He's out searching, son, – oh, it's you, Angus, isn't it?" It was the tall policeman from yesterday. "What's wrong?" Angus tried not to babble as he explained about delivering catalogues and the house where he'd seen

Janet and Mr Beuglehole.

"Okay, mate, let me talk to the boss. It's likely we already know about the house but I'll check." He went out the back and returned after a few minutes with a burly police sergeant who made Angus repeat his story.

The sergeant peered down at Angus. "And you're quite sure it was this Janet character and Beuglehole?"

"Yes, definitely, Janet spoke to me before driving away." Angus couldn't understand why they weren't racing around to the house immediately.

"Look, son, at this stage we think it's unlikely they've got Ben. There's been no demand for money and he's run off before. I'm reluctant to pull busy police off the search but I suppose we should take a look, at least. What's the exact address?"

But Angus didn't know the exact address. He couldn't even remember the name of the street, he'd walked up and down so many that day.

"Can you direct us there?" said the Sergeant.

"Yes, I can show you, no problem."

"Okay, let's go."

Angus was too worried about Ben to enjoy the total epicness (a word he made up later) of riding in the back of a police car to what was likely to be the bad-guys' hide-out. He hoped he'd get to see Beuglehole arrested. Three minutes later they were at the house, pulling straight into the empty driveway.

"Stay in the car." Angus chewed his bottom lip anxiously and watched the two police officers walk up to the house and knock at the door. When a second knock went unanswered they went around the back. A few minutes later they returned to the car and got in.

"There's no one here, son," said the Sergeant, gruffly, before starting the car.

"But how do you know?" said Angus, "Just because no one answered the door—"

"Because the back was open and we walked through the place," said the Sergeant. "It was empty and we've wasted enough time here." He spoke quite harshly and Angus remained silent on the ride back.

At the center the sergeant strode off without another word but the other guy said, "Don't feel bad. It was a good idea. We'll go through the place again, looking for more evidence of what those two have been up to. But Ben's not there so it's not an immediate priority."

Angus rode home feeling embarrassed and deflated. The police sergeant had been annoyed with him for wasting their time, and wasting their time was the last thing he'd wanted to do. He'd been sure Ben would be there.

He went to his room and tried Skyping Hamish and Bodhi but neither answered. Just for something to do, he flicked through the video footage and stills they'd taken at Scream House in preparation for filming the zombie movie.

It really was a scary looking yard. He looked at the overgrown bushes, the broken birdbath, the old wishing well, the bomb shelter, the – wait – the *bomb shelter*. He swiped back to the previous photo. Angus had leaned over the fence to take the picture but it wasn't a good shot. Only a bit of the trap door to the shelter was captured. He hadn't bothered to take another since Mrs Screen had said they couldn't use it for filming. The brass padlock could just be seen in the corner.

Hmmm…A shiny new brass padlock, even though Mrs Screen said the shelter hadn't been used in years. He remembered thinking the grass looked trampled down around the hatch, too. He peered at the photo to examine the grass again but it was difficult to tell. Angus quickly flicked through the other photos but, as he thought, there were no more of the bomb shelter hatch.

He put down his iPad.

Could Ben be in the bomb-shelter?

Of course he could! But wouldn't the police have checked it? No, he didn't think they would have. The old bomb shelter was no longer in the Scream House yard, so the police wouldn't even know about it unless someone had told them. And who was there to tell? Mrs Screen was in hospital and may not have thought of it anyway, and Mr Jackson probably didn't even know it existed.

Angus jumped up.

He had to tell the police. *Wrong*. How would he do that, exactly? Insist he had a new theory? Say he was sure he was right this time? They'd laugh at him, and what if he actually convinced them to check it out and Ben wasn't there? He'd look like a total idiot, *again*.

No, he'd check this one out himself.

22 BEN

He flew down the stairs, planning to tell his mother that he had to check something out at Scream House. But she spoke first. "Your father just called. They police have received a ransom demand. Janet and that man *have* got Ben. You were right. They want five million dollars to give him back, they say – Angus! Where are you going?"

He was out the door and on his bike before his

mother could tell him not to go. This *was* an emergency. He'd deal with consequences later. He pedalled fast, his heart thumping madly. It was just on dark and the street lamps cast a yellow glow over the path while a flock of lorikeets screeched in deafening unison from the trees above.

As he pedalled, he tried to come up with a plan. He knew the police were at Scream House, fingerprinting. Now that a ransom demand had been received surely they'd be keen to check the bomb shelter.

At Scream House, he dumped his bike and ducked beneath the blue and white police tape. At the front door he knocked loudly and called out. There was no answer. There didn't seem to be anyone there. Everything was quiet and the lights were out. He ran to the kitchen door and realised there hadn't been any police cars or vans out the front. Maybe they'd finished their work or maybe they'd all been diverted to work on the ransom demand. No answer at that door, either.

He looked at the garden. It was quite dark now but the moon was out. At night the yard looked creepier than ever with the bushes and trees casting deep pockets of shadow, their spidery branches reaching and clawing at the air.

His feet moved from the path and into the garden. They were taking him toward the bomb shelter. He'd have a look for himself. See if there was anything to see before going to the police and possibly looking stupid again if there was nothing there. He brushed against a branch and something scuttled across his cheek. A spider? Swallowing a scream, he smacked the thing away and kept going.

The moon disappeared behind a cloud and the night became as black as ink. Unable to see a thing, Angus stood in the dark for about thirty seconds, listening to his heart thud. Then the moon returned and he kept moving.

At the fence, he checked his bearings to make sure he was in the correct part of the garden. It was harder to tell at night. On his left stood the ring of toadstools where Mrs Screen and her daughter had played, so yes, this was it. He stood up on the bottom railing and peered over. At first he couldn't see the hatch or the brass lock and wondered if he was, in fact, in the wrong place. Then something glinted in the moonlight. The lock! The hatch had been covered by what looked like clumps of weeds, making it almost impossible to see. He needed to get a better look.

Rather than climb the fence and risk making a noise

jumping down, he followed it around to the front gate, went out onto the street and into the neighbourless block next door, following the fence again back to the bomb shelter. Now on the same side, he crouched to get a better look.

The padlock was undone.

Still crouching, Angus leant against the fence to consider what to do next when it suddenly gave way. *What the…?* Just managing not to lose his balance and fall on his broken arm, he steadied himself and tried to understand what had just happened. It seemed the bottom section of fence just here was actually a separate piece, attached with double hinges so that it swung both in and out. There had been no need for him to have walked out to the street to get to this side of the fence. All anyone had to do was push on the lower part in the right place and the panel would swing back allowing them to crawl through.

In the stillness of the night, Angus heard a sound. Very faintly, he could hear a child crying. *Ben!*

With his heart threatening to break through his ribcage, he lifted back the hatch. The crying was instantly louder. Steps led down into the ground and he could see light at the bottom. Although he desperately wanted to call out Ben's name he managed not to. What if *they* were down there, too? He listened. All he could hear was crying. He placed a foot on the top step, then the other on the next step. Before he knew it, he was three steps in.

Now he could see Ben. He was sitting on a stretcher bed against the wall, his face screwed up with misery, eyes shut yet tears spilling down his small cheeks. Angus was about to call out when someone appeared from the other side of the shelter. *Janet!*

"Stop that noise, you little brat, or I'll give you something to cry about." She strode toward Ben, her back to Angus and the steps. "Here, eat this," she said, holding out a plate with a sandwich on it.

Ben opened his eyes and immediately saw Angus on the steps. His mouth opened in surprise and Angus quickly held a finger to his lips. *Be quiet, Ben*. Ben shut his mouth again and looked at the sandwich. He was a clever kid. He knew not to draw Janet's attention to Angus.

Angus backed up the stairs slowly and now held his finger up, hoping Ben would understand that it meant he'd be back soon with help. He would run to the center and tell them he'd found Ben. They'd have to listen.

He'd scream and scream until they did.

Janet left the sandwich with Ben and withdrew to the far corner of the shelter, out of sight. Angus had one step to go when his foot slipped and scraped against the wall.

"What was that?" Oh no! Janet had heard. Angus froze but clever Ben immediately hurled his sandwich to the ground, the plate clanging on the floor, and began wailing loudly. He was causing a distraction so Angus could get away.

He fled out the opening and quickly shut the hatch. The fastest way to the center would be through the yard of Scream House and out the back gate.

He pushed at the fence panel but strong hands grabbed him from behind and yanked him backwards.

23 ESCAPE

Before he could scream, a hand clamped hard over his mouth and dragged him up, forcing his good arm up behind his back.

"Mr Adams," said Beuglehole, "how lovely of you to visit. Don't rush off." Beuglehole kicked open the hatch and forced Angus down the steps. "Look what I found outside."

Janet gaped in surprise. Ben saw what was happening

and began crying even louder.

"For God's sake, shut that kid up," said Beuglehole.

"How do you expect me to do that, exactly?" said Janet, but Beuglehole ignored her. He took his hand away from Angus's mouth and grabbed at some rope on a shelf.

"Help me tie him up. I told you this interfering brat would be trouble."

"Well, we needed him, didn't we?" said Janet, taking the end of the rope. "How else were we supposed to know what Jackson was thinking? We had to know if the plan was working."

So Janet had been friendly to Angus in the hope of finding out what Mr Jackson was thinking; hoping to hear that he was still angry at Mrs Screen and that all their dirty tricks were working.

Angus wasn't sure what to do now. If he stomped on Beuglehole's foot and actually managed to get away, they'd likely be gone with Ben by the time he returned with the police.

"You won't get away with this," he said, even though he knew it was lame. "The police know you're here."

"Be quiet or I'll tape your mouth shut," said Beuglehole, pulling Angus's sling off his broken wrist and casting it aside. He roughly pulled both arms behind Angus's back and tied them together before pushing him down onto the stretcher.

"What about him?" said Janet, looking at Ben. "Shouldn't we tie him too while we go see Greg? You did ring my brother, right? He'd better have the new passports ready."

So, they were planning to leave the country.

"Shut up, you fool!" Mr Beuglehole threw his hands into the air. He glared at Janet with narrowed eyes, his face turning red. Angus had seen this often enough at school. Mr Beuglehole was furious. Through gritted teeth he said, "We can't let these brats go now. You've just told them the plan!"

Janet stammered and spluttered but Beuglehole only told her to hurry and tie up Ben. "Right," said Beuglehole, looking at them both on the stretcher. "They'll be safe enough until we get back. We'll have to work out where to dump them once we get the money." They hurried up the steps and out the hatch. The padlock clicked shut.

"It's alright, Ben, I'm not going to let them hurt you. We'll find a way out."

Ben was no longer howling but crying silently, his

cheeks wet with tears. “Daddy,” he said, softly.

“It’s so great to hear you talk, mate. I’m going to get you to your Dad, don’t worry.”

Angus tried wriggling his arms but they were tied tight. “You’ve been very brave and clever, you know. Now, I need you to help me find something sharp to cut these ropes.”

Ben stopped crying and they both looked around. There had to be something sharp in here. Angus stood up and went to the shelves. There were rows and rows of old canned food because, of course, this was an old bomb shelter. People had stored food and water in case they were stuck in here for a while. An idea occurred to him. If there was food then maybe there’d be knives and forks. He told Ben what they had to look for.

With their hands behind their backs they searched as best they could. Apart from food, the shelves held old kerosene lanterns, boxes of matches, tin mugs and plates, and musty-smelling blankets. Strangely, there wasn’t cutlery of any kind. Some old crates were stacked in the corner.

“Look out, Ben. I’m going to knock these over and tip out whatever’s in them.” Using his shoulder, Angus pushed the top crate onto the floor with a crash. Pay dirt.

Out spilled knives, forks, spoons, and assorted cooking utensils. Angus quickly found what he'd been hoping for: a small, sharp paring knife.

Awkwardly, he squatted down with his back to the knife, just managing to pick it up with his hands tied behind his back. He told Ben to sit on the floor. He didn't know how long they would have until Janet and Beuglehole returned so there was no time to waste.

Angus sat on the floor back-to-back with Ben. "I'm going to cut through the rope that's tying your wrists together, Ben. I'll be very careful, don't worry. You need to keep very still. Do you understand?" With their heads both turned, Angus saw Ben give a nod. "Okay, here I go."

The knife was sharp. Ben sat perfectly still. Angus felt carefully with his fingers and slid the knife in under the rope on Ben's wrists. He worked it back and forth and in only a couple of minutes it was cut through. Ben jumped up, grinning, and clapped his hands together.

"Now, Ben, you have to cut my rope. Do you think you can?" Ben nodded and with a serious face took the knife and knelt down at Angus's back. "Slide it under with the sharp edge toward the rope. Be careful not to cut yourself. Now move the knife back and forth, pushing it into the rope."

Ben was slower at cutting than Angus, who fought the urge to tell him to hurry up. He didn't want to stress Ben or risk him cutting himself with the knife. Beads of sweat began to form on Angus's forehead. It wasn't particularly hot in the shelter, but he was terrified they were running out of time. Finally, he felt the rope snap and his hands were free.

"Awesome! Great job, Ben." He jumped up, ran up to the hatch, and pushed hard. Of course it was locked. Angus studied it. Two hinges attached it to the roof of the shelter. "Ben, look for a screwdriver!"

They found one in the mess of cutlery. Angus raced back to the hatch. The screws were old and rusty and undoing them was hard going. He had to stand on the steps and reach awkwardly over his head. He dropped the screwdriver twice because of sweaty hands. Desperate to escape, and close to panic, he forced himself to breathe slowly and concentrate.

One by one, the screws came out. When the last of them fell to the ground, Angus pushed the hatch back and felt the cool night breeze on his face. "Quickly, Ben, let's go." He climbed out and Ben followed. "Now we have to crawl through here. You first." Angus held up the fence panel and Ben scurried underneath. Angus put his own head through. Wait – what was that? There was movement in the bushes.

Janet and Beuglehole were back.

24 *RUN!*

"**G**et them!" Steel-cold fingers grabbed hold of his ankle. Angus kicked hard with his other foot and connected with something that felt like bone. Beuglehole swore and let go.

Angus scrambled through, grabbed Ben's hand and they took off, leaving Beuglehole shouting an order at Janet to hide near the front gate. He was coming after them.

There was more swearing. Beuglehole had tripped over a toadstool. *Thank you, fairies.*

Angus used his injured arm to pull Ben through the garden, branches and bushes striking his face despite using his good arm as a shield. Something sharp scratched his forehead. He touched it and felt wetness. He was bleeding.

The overgrown garden gave them the advantage of cover but made it impossible to run very fast, particularly with a small, terrified boy in tow. Thrashing sounds from behind meant Beuglehole was close.

Then the moon disappeared and blackness enveloped everything. Angus couldn't see, but he knew the direction they needed to go so he tried to keep moving forward, feeling about with his good arm, clutching Ben's hand tightly with the other. At least Beuglehole would also be in darkness.

Ben tripped and stumbled, let go of Angus, and cried out as he hit the ground. Angus felt for him quickly and grabbed his hand. Beuglehole was right behind them. "Come on, Ben, you have to get up!" he whispered, urgently. Ben tried, but cried out again and sank back. He must have sprained an ankle or something.

The moon was slowly reappearing. Angus grabbed

Ben under the arms and pulled him behind a large oleander bush just as the garden was flooded in moonlight. Two seconds later, Beuglehole blundered past, not seeing them, still charging toward the back gate, clearly believing the boys to be ahead of him.

What to do? It was no good carrying Ben back to the street because Janet had been left there to wait. And he couldn't carry him down to the rear gate because they'd be sure to run into Beuglehole, who was likely to come back any minute when he realised they hadn't made it out.

He looked around and saw the old wishing well. Whispering reassurances, he carried Ben to it, lifted him over the side, and then climbed in himself. Together, they crouched against the low wall.

"We'll hide here until they go, Ben. If we stay really quiet it'll be okay." Angus wasn't at all sure that it was going to be okay but this was the best he could do. Beside him Ben clutched his clammy hand tightly but didn't make a sound. Even his breathing was quiet. He was being incredibly brave. What horror this little five-year-old had endured. He'd been kidnapped, kept prisoner, tied up, and now chased through this jungle of a yard by a mad-man with only Angus to protect him.

Angus squeezed his hand. He was doing his best but would his best be good enough?

There was rustling in the nearby shrubs. Beuglehole was back.

Terrified, Angus listened to twigs and dry grass crunching underfoot as the man came closer. Creepily, Beuglehole began murmuring in a sweet, sing-songy voice.

"I know you're here, boys. I heard one of you cry out before and I know you didn't make it to the gate."

The footsteps stopped. He was listening for them.

"Is one of you hurt? Well, we can't have that, can we? Come out now, like good boys, and we'll fix up that nasty ouchy."

Angus held his finger to his lips to let Ben know he must be absolutely quiet. Ben squeezed his hand. After a few seconds the crunching noises started again and slowly became louder. He was heading toward them.

"Just look at this lovely wishing well. I wonder what I should wish for?" He was directly on the other side of the wall. If he leaned over he'd see them.

Ben whimpered.

"GOTCHA!" Beuglehole lunged his upper body over the wall. Angus leapt up, raised his broken arm and smashed the heavy cast into the man's face. Beuglehole fell backward.

"Come on, Ben!" Angus quickly got them both out of the well. Beuglehole lay flat on his back, unmoving. Was he dead? Angus wasn't about to hang around and find out. Who knew how long it would be before Janet came to investigate.

"Want a piggy-back, Ben?"

With his wrist aching and his face scratched and bloody, he carried Ben on his back through the remainder of the garden, the little boy's hands clasped tightly around his neck, his face buried in Angus's back. Once he'd cleared the back gate he jogged across the playing field to the community center, telling Ben he was safe now.

He stumbled through the front door, panting. The police, huddled around desks and telephones, all looked up and stared.

"I've found Ben," he said. For a moment there was absolute silence. Then someone at the back yelled.

"*BEN*!" Mr Jackson pushed his way through past the police, scooped Ben up from Angus's back, and wept.

***

Beuglehole wasn't dead, just unconscious. Angus's

cast had got him right in the middle of his forehead and he'd have a nasty headache when he woke up. The police sent him to hospital under guard.

Janet had been caught at her brother's house. When Beuglehole didn't come back she went looking, found him on the ground, and fled. After an all-night police interview she confessed to everything.

Most shocking was the confession that not only were they fraudsters but murderers, too. They'd killed Mrs Screen's daughter (Ben's mother and Mr Jackson's wife) by tampering with the brakes of her car so she'd crash. Then they set about making sure that Mrs Screen and Mr Jackson stayed angry and upset at each other, until they could convince her to leave all of her money to Janet and *not* Mr Jackson or Ben.

When Mrs Screen said she wanted to make amends with Mr Jackson they knew they had to hurry up their plan. Beuglehole (who *was* actually a teacher) had started working at the school and realised he had access to the poison they needed to kill Mrs Screen. And it had almost worked.

Mrs Screen, still in hospital but recovering well, insisted on buying Angus a new high-definition video camera. Angus said it wasn't necessary, but she insisted.

She said it had been her employee who'd broken the last one so that was that.

She also told him he'd better hurry up and do his filming at Scream House because it wouldn't be scary for much longer. It was time to start spending some of her money fixing the place up, she said, and making it beautiful again for Ben. The first job would be to chop down that dangerous ironbark. She and Ben were going to plant a new tree in memory of his mother.

Angus got a Band-Aid for his scratched forehead and a new plaster cast for his arm. His mother suggested that since this was now his third one, perhaps he could try to *not* smash it into any faces. He said he'd do his best.

25 AND THE WINNER IS...

Hamish leaned forward. “Hey, pass the popcorn.” Angus handed the jumbo sized tub to Liam, who passed it to Bodhi, who passed it to Hamish. “Thanks,” he said, cramming a handful into his mouth, and spilling more down his shirt.

At the front of the hall, the credits rolled across the screen for yet another lip-synced Taylor Swift video. Angus clapped politely as the category winner was announced.

"Had the worst dream last night," said Hamish, still chewing. "Instead of playing our movie, they showed a video of me naked in the bath from when I was two."

"That wasn't just a dream. I spoke to your mother and it's coming up next. I thought it couldn't hurt to enter a comedy," said Angus.

Finn, in the row ahead, turned around. "Speaking of Hamish and comedies." He held up his phone. There on the screen was Hamish on stage, his kilt in full swirl as he kicked and twirled his way through the Highland Fling. He wasn't bad.

"Hey! What? How?" he spluttered, trying to grab the phone, but Finn was too fast.

"I've got one word for you. Facebook. Or is that two words?" Finn grinned and turned around.

Hamish sighed. "I'm going to kill my mother."

"Shhh, we're up next," whispered Bodhi.

Their movie looked good on the big screen. The zombies were truly hideous and the audience gasped and laughed in all the right places. Scream House added a touch of brilliance. Angus had edited in some lighting effects that made the garden spookier than ever. Even Finn jumped in his seat when a zombie sprang up out of the bomb shelter (*thanks, Mrs Screen*). The final scene was a triumph. The homemade green screen, that was really pink, had worked brilliantly. The audience cheered as Angus tricked the zombies into the giant lizard enclosure where they were chased and eaten (the eating part was left to the imagination but everyone seemed to get it). The credits rolled to loud applause.

"We're going to win this," whispered Hamish. "I can feel it in my waters."

Angus rolled his eyes. "Have your waters ever been right?"

"Yeah. Last week. When we sorted out, Liam's…er…problem."

Angus nodded. "True."

Finn and Luke's spy comedy was shown next. It was funny. So funny that Angus was secretly worried it might just beat them. But he was wrong. In the end, neither video won. 'Best Movie' went to a serious film about a girl trying to make friends at a new school.

"Horror and comedy are never given the same level of respect as serious drama," said Bodhi, knowledgably. "No one cares that they're just as difficult to make. More so, probably."

"Ripped off," said Hamish in disgust. "That movie

was so boring I nearly fell asleep."

But the night wasn't a total loss. In an upset, Liam beat the favourite to take out 'Best Supporting Actor – Junior School'. He walked up to the stage with confidence and a beaming smile.

"Good to see him back to his old self again," said Hamish.

Angus clapped until his hands hurt.

26 THE WEEK BEFORE

Rapata sauntered around the corner of the art block. He was on time. Angus took a deep breath. He was sweating, and not just because he was hot under the thick pullover. The air carried the muted sounds of children playing elsewhere in the school. No one ever came to this quiet back corner.

It was perfect.

Rapata passed the hedge, startling a magpie hunting

grubs. He stopped in front of Angus.

"Okay, Adams. I'm here. Whaddya want?"

"I want you to leave my brother and his friends alone."

Rapata snorted. "Make me."

"So you admit it? You've been forcing Liam to give you his food and money?"

"Like takin' candy from a baby. Ya see, he's weak like you, Adams. Yer a couple a losers."

"What about trashing the school's green screen? Did you really think you'd get away with it?"

Rapata shrugged. "But I did get away with it. Yer boring me, Adams. Get outa my way or I'll give ya a busted rib to go with the arm."

Angus stepped forward, his face now an inch from Rapata's chest. Staring straight up into dull eyes he said, slowly and loudly, "I'm telling you *now* to stop bullying my brother. You got it?"

Rapata tilted his head to one side very slightly, as though trying to comprehend this unexpected turn of events. Nobody stood up to him. Ever.

The smirk widened. "You're stupider than I thought, Adams." With unlikely speed he smashed a fist into Angus's stomach. Angus cried out and fell to the ground. He drew his knees up, protectively, and looked at Rapata's shoes. They needed a good polish.

One of the unpolished shoes drew back. A kick was coming. Angus quickly rolled and the shoe drove into his back.

"Like I said. A loser." Rapata stepped over him. "You're gettin' fat, too. You wanna watch that. Bad for ya health. Tell ya brother, I'll see him tomorrow." He walked away, laughing.

Angus stood up. "Did you get it?"

Hamish and Bodhi came from behind the hedge. Angus took off his pullover and Hamish helped him to untie the cushions strapped across his stomach and back.

Bodhi looked down at the camera. "It's all here," she said,

***

The home bell was ringing when they left the principal's office the following afternoon. Together, the three of them went to collect their school bags.

"Well, good riddance to Rapata," said Bodhi.

Hamish gave a low whistle. "Expelled. Crikey. I mean, I thought he'd get a suspension, but...*expelled*?"

"It's not like he didn't deserve it," said Angus. "And you heard Mr Dingwall, he's had previous warnings."

He sighed. “It’s one less thing to worry about, anyway.”

“I knew it’d all work out, of course,” said Hamish, brightly. “I felt it in my waters.”

“Sure you did,” said Angus.

Bodhi looked at Hamish. “You do know what that means, don’t you? What ‘waters’ refers to?”

Hamish looked blank. “Not really.”

“It means ‘pee’. You’re saying you felt it in your *pee*.”

Angus took a step away. “Dude, that is so gross.”

Hamish frowned. “Are you sure?”

“To be on the safe side,” said Bodhi, touching his shoulder, “why don’t you just say ‘I can feel it in my *bones*’ like everyone else.”

“Because my bones don’t feel anything. It’s all in my water, I tell you.”

“You guys go ahead, I’ll catch up,” said Angus. “I suddenly need to use the bathroom.”

The End

HAVE YOU READ ALL OF THE FREE-RANGE KID MYSTERIES?

Angus Adams and the Free-Range Kid Mysteries (Book 1)

Angus Adams and the Missing Pro Surfer (Book 2)

Angus Adams and Scream House (Book 3)

Email Lee. M. Winter: lee@leemwinter.com

CPSIA information can be obtained
at www.ICGtesting.com
Printed in the USA
BVHW040241011118
531862BV00001B/67/P